£5-

Published in Great Britain 1986 by
Webb & Bower (Publishers) Limited
9 Colleton Crescent, Exeter, Devon EX2 4BY
in association with Michael Joseph Limited, 27 Wright's Lane, London W8 5TZ
Production Nick Facer

First published in dossier form 1937 by Hutchinson & Co (Publishers) Limited
Republished in facsimile form 1980 by Webb & Bower (Publishers) Limited
This edition Copyright © Webb & Bower (Publishers) Limited 1986

British Library Cataloguing in Publication Data
Wheatley, Dennis
  Murder off Miami
  1. Title 2. Links, J.G.
  823'.912[F]   PR6045.   H127

  ISBN 0-86350-118-4

Printed and bound in Hong Kong by Mandarin Offset Marketing (HK) Limited

Jacket design
The jacket for this book was designed by Peta Baskerville,
Creative Director of Proteus Design Ltd., using a Dicomed
Imaginator Computer Graphics Design Station.

FORM NO. 6D.

WESTERN UNION
(THE WESTERN UNION TELEGRAPH COMPANY)
CABLEGRAM

ANGLO-AMERICAN TELEGRAPH Co., Ld.   CANADIAN NATIONAL TELEGRAPHS.

-8 MAR.36

S Y GOLDENGULL MIAMIRADIO 13 8 2045

POLICE HEADQUARTERS MIAMIFLA =

BOLITHO BLANE COMMITTED SUICIDE STOP

RETURNING PORT IMMEDIATELY STOP =

ROCKSAVAGE +

Police Department.
Form GO/7431/N 58

POLICE HEADQUARTERS,

MIAMI,

FLA.

9.20 p.m.   8.3.36.

MEMO.

To Detective Officer Kettering.

Radiogram herewith passed to you for attention.
Bolitho Blane is a British financier.   The yacht Golden
Gull left Miami Beach at 7 o'clock this evening. As she
was an hour and three quarters out when radio was despatched
she should be in about 10.30 p.m.

Meet yacht and undertake investigation.

John Milton Schwab

Lieutenant
Florida Police.

REPORT OF DETECTIVE OFFICER KETTERING OF THE FLORIDA POLICE.

Acting on instructions received I boarded S.Y. Golden Gull from police launch X21. at 10.40 p.m. in the company of Detective Officer Neame, Police Surgeon Jacket, Station Photographer Southwold and Officer Gurdon of the Uniform Branch.

Captain Derringham received me with the owner, Mr. Carlton Rocksavage.   I proceeded to the Captain's cabin to take statements, Detective Officer Neame acting as stenographer.

CAPTAIN DERRINGHAM'S STATEMENT.

We sailed from New York at 12.30 p.m. on the 5th carrying five passengers in addition to the owner, Mr. Carlton Rocksavage, and his daughter, Miss Ferri Rocksavage.   The passengers were Lady Welter, the Honourable Reginald Jocelyn and Mrs. Jocelyn, who are Lady Welter's daughter and son-in-law, the Bishop of Bude and Count Luigi Posodini.

We arrived off Miami at 2.35 p.m. this afternoon, where we anchored.   My instructions were that three new guests would come on and, immediately these were aboard, I was to proceed to Nassau Bahamas.

At 4.30 p.m. a Japanese gentleman, Mr. Inosuke Hayashi came on board and at 6.55 Mr. Bolitho Blane, accompanied by his secretary, Nicholas Stodart.   The tender was cleared by 7.5, upon which I gave orders that the ship should proceed to sea.

At 8.38, just after I had sat down to dinner in my cabin, I was sent for by the owner to come down to the suite which had been

allotted to Mr. Bolitho Blane.   I found the owner there with Mr.
Blane's secretary.   They explained to me that Mr. Blane was
missing and had left a note which gave reason to suppose that he
had committed suicide.   The window of the drawing room cabin was
wide open and it looked as if Mr. Blane had thrown himself overboard through it.

It was decided not to alarm the other passengers so the
owner said that he would just tell them that Mr. Blane was ill and
we were returning to Miami for a doctor.   At 8.45 I ordered the
ship back to port.

MR. CARLTON ROCKSAVAGE'S STATEMENT.

We had just come down from New York for a few days' pleasure
cruising off the islands, and I had arranged to pick up two more
of my guests who could not make the yacht at New York, from Miami.

Mr. Inosuke Hayashi came on during the afternoon and had tea
with us, then Mr. Bolitho Blane arrived with his secretary,
Nicholas Stodart, just before 7 o'clock.   They went straight down
to the private suite which I had allotted to them, and we sailed
at once.

I didn't see them as I was on the bridge with my Captain
when we left Miami at 7.5.   Then I went down to the lounge for a
drink and, finding Pamela Jocelyn and Count Posodini there, I
talked with them for a while.

At 7.25 Mr. Stodart arrived and introduced himself as
Bolitho Blane's secretary.   He said that Blane wished to get some

CARLTON ROCKSAVAGE.   RETAKE FROM PHOTOGRAPH IN LOUNGE.   9.3.36.

cables off before changing and asked that I would excuse him from putting in an appearance before dinner.

I introduced Stodart to Mrs. Jocelyn and the Count, then offered him a drink which he accepted. After a few moments Stodart asked me if the type sheets on the notice board in the lounge contained the closing prices of the New York stock market and, on my telling him that that was so, he said that Mr. Blane was anxious to have the latest information. He took down some of the prices in his note book, tore the leaf out and, as he had not finished his drink, asked the lounge steward to take the list down to Blane's cabin.

The steward came up again and said that the drawing room of Blane's suite was locked and that he could get no answer.

Stodart then told him to take it down again and slip it under the door.

Mrs. Jocelyn and Count Posodini left us at about this time and I remained with Stodart for a while. Later, the Bishop joined us and Lady Welter came in a few minutes after him. Then I noticed that it was already ten after eight, so realising that I would have to hurry, if I were not to be late for dinner, I went down to change.

At a little after 8.30 I got back to the lounge to find all my guests assembled for dinner, except Bolitho Blane and Stodart. Just as I was contemplating sending down a message to Blane, the cabin steward came up with an urgent request that I should go down to Blane's cabin right away.

On arriving there I found Stodart standing in the drawing room looking very pale and shaken.   He said to me, "Mr. Rock-savage, I'm afraid I've got bad news for you."   Then he handed me this note

Dear Stodart,

You know how worried I've been all through the trip over. Day after day I've been watching Argus Shares go down as the bears slammed into them. I had hoped to pull my companies through but things have gone too far for Rockesavage to give me a decent deal, so I am past caring what happens to them now.

This party was a forlorn hope and I never wanted to join it. There's a tough crowd behind Rockesavage, and I wouldn't put it past them to try and do me in while I'm on this yacht. That would send the Argus shares down to zero without any further argument. Anyhow, I'm not going to wait and chance it. The struggle has proved too much for me. I have always loathed publicity and rather than face the nightmare of a bankruptcy examination I'm clearing out.

Robert Blair

MR. CARLTON ROCKSAVAGE'S STATEMENT, CONTINUED.

What he says in that note about there being a tough crowd behind me is sheer nonsense.   Just a wild statement of a man who was half off his head with worry.   He didn't know the first thing about me personally as we had never even met and, as I didn't see him when he came on board, I never set eyes on the man in my life.

We had corresponded a lot in a business way, of course, and I knew that he had been having a tough time lately, so I was hoping that this little trip, with a few nice people, right away from everything, was just what he needed to set him up again, and I was looking forward to making his acquaintance.

After I had read that letter I've just given you, Stodart handed me a slip of paper which, he said, the cabin steward had found on Blane's table.   I saw at once that it was the page that Stodart had torn out of his pocket book after he had taken down the quotations of the closing prices of the New York stock market from the notice board in the lounge and which he had sent down to Blane earlier on.   It had a few lines of writing in a different hand on the other side.   Here it is ....

Police Department.
Form RL/2120/C.7.

LEAF TORN FROM STODART'S POCKET BOOK AT 7.40 p.m. 8.3.36. AND

FOUND BY CABIN STEWARD IN BOLITHO BLANE'S CABIN AT 8.33 p.m.

MARCH, 1936

8 SUNDAY (68—298)
Full Moon 5-14 a m.

Redmeyer Synd 66³/₁₆ - 66³/₄

Denton Bros Inc 84½ - 85

Rocksarage Con 51³/₄ - 52/₁₆

Grandol Soaps 93 - 92⁵/₁₆

Argus Suds 39³/₄ - 39½

Sea Toilet Preps 72 - 77¼

N. S.

MARCH, 1936

9 MONDAY (69—297)

Yes sir! Are you keeping under 40.
So the game is up

MR. CARLTON ROCKSAVAGE'S STATEMENT, CONTINUED.

I sent for the Captain at once, told him what had occurred and he put back to port, while I sent a message up to my daughter that she was to take the guests in to dinner, then went up to the wireless room and sent a radio to the Miami police.

MR. NICHOLAS STODART'S STATEMENT.

Mr. Blane told me about a fortnight ago that his companies were in very serious difficulties but that his principal competitor, Mr. Carlton Rocksavage, had invited him to a conference in the United States.   Mr. Blane believed that Mr. Rocksavage's companies were in almost as serious difficulties as his own, owing to the price cutting war which had been going on between them for a considerable time.

Mr. Blane was the big man of the British soap combine and Mr. Rocksavage the head of the rival group in America.   Between them they could have had the virtual control of the world soap market, but they have been trying to smash each other for months past and neither has succeeded to date.   That cost both groups an immense amount of money, and an amalgamation between them would have meant salvation to them both, whereas, if they continued their rivalry, it was quite certain that one of them would go under.

Mr. Blane accepted Mr. Rocksavage's invitation and we sailed for the United States in the Berengaria.   During the voyage Mr. Blane was very depressed.   The steady fall in the shares of his

NICHOLAS STODART.   FLASHED BY DETECTIVE OFFICER NEAME.   9.3.36.

companies caused him grave anxiety and he told me repeatedly that
if Argus Suds went below 45 he would have very little chance of
pulling off a deal with Rocksavage except upon ruinous terms and
that, if Argus Suds went below 40, there would be no chance of his
pulling off a deal at all, as it would pay Rocksavage better, in
that case, to let him go under.   The fact that the shares of the
Rocksavage companies were also falling, although in a lesser
degree, did not appear to console him.

Mr. Blane's depression was so great at times that I had
grave doubts as to his sanity.   He seemed to think that
Rocksavage and his associates would stop at nothing to wreck him.
He knew, of course, that his death would mean a complete slump in
the Blane interests and, although he had never met Mr. Rocksavage,
he apparently regarded him as a man who might even go the length
of engineering his death in order to smash the Blane companies.

He knew that his only hope of pulling his companies through
was this conference on the Golden Gull, yet he seemed to think
that by going on board he would be taking his life in his hands,
and it was such statements as these which made me consider him to
be off his mental balance at times.

We could have joined the yacht in New York, but Blane jibbed
at the last moment from this fear that his life would be in
jeopardy, but he pulled himself together a few hours later and I
cabled Mr. Rocksavage for him that we would fly down to join the
yacht at Miami.

Just before 7 o'clock we came out to the yacht in a tender

and, on being told that Mr. Rocksavage was on the bridge, went straight down to our suite with the chief steward. The cabin steward came along and asked if he could unpack, but Mr. Blane was so nervous that he would not allow the man inside his cabin. The yacht got under way just about then and Mr. Blane told me to change at once and, when I left him, he was starting to unpack his things himself.

Directly I had changed I returned to the drawing room and found Mr. Blane had only unpacked a few things from his suitcase. He was sitting staring out of the porthole window. After a moment he sent me up to Mr. Rocksavage with a message that he wished to get some cables off, and so would not appear before dinner, and told me at the same time that I was to get the latest market prices which had come in by radio and send them down to him.

That was at 7.30. I went straight up to the lounge, and, finding Mr. Rocksavage there, introduced myself to him. He introduced me to Mrs. Jocelyn and Count Posodini, and gave me a drink. I took down the closing prices in which Mr. Blane was interested. These were sent down at 7.40 by the lounge steward, who returned to say that Mr. Blane's door was locked and that he could get no reply. I remarked that Mr. Blane would be changing and was probably in his bath, so the steward was instructed to slip the note under his cabin door.

Mrs. Jocelyn and Count Posodini left us just after that and I remained in the lounge talking to Mr. Rocksavage. The Bishop

of Bude came in and then Lady Welter.   Mr. Rocksavage remarked
shortly after that it was ten past eight, so he must change at
once or he would be late, and if he was we were to go in to dinner
without him.

After he had left us Mr. Inosuke Hayashi came in, then Count
Posodini.   At 8.30 Mrs. Jocelyn, having changed, returned to the
lounge with her husband, Mr. Reggie Jocelyn, to whom she
introduced me.

It was just after the dinner bugle sounded that the cabin
steward came up to the lounge and handed me the note that Mr.
Blane had left for me.

Having read it I hurried below with the cabin steward.   We
found that Mr. Blane's suite was empty and the window of his
drawing room wide open, so it looked as though he had thrown
himself out into the sea.   It was then that the steward picked up
a piece of paper from the writing table, which I recognised at
once as the leaf from my pocket book with the share quotations on
it, and I saw the line of writing in Blane's hand containing his
last message on the back of it.   I sent the steward up to get
Mr. Rocksavage at once and, immediately I had told him what had
occurred, he sent for the Captain.

This business has been a great shock to me because, although
I have not been in Mr. Blane's employ for very long, he always
treated me decently and I had got to be very fond of him.   I don't
think there is the least doubt about it being a case of suicide.
Big business people may use unscrupulous methods at times but it's

stretching things a bit too far to suggest that they actually
murder one another.   I think Mr. Blane's fear for his life was
brought on purely by an overstrained imagination and, realising
that his last hope of saving his companies had disappeared, when
the Argus Suds shares dropped below the 40 level, he decided to
make an end of himself rather than face the music.

STATEMENT OF SILAS RINGBOTTOM, CABIN STEWARD.

Just before the ship got under way the chief steward called
for me and said, "Ringbottom the two new ones that are allotted
to suite C. have just come aboard.   Get along at once and settle
them in."

I went to C. drawing room and knocked on the door.   The
secretary opened it and I asked, "Shall I unpack, sir?" and he
replied, "No, that's all right. We're unpacking for ourselves."
So I went back to my pantry.

I did one or two odd jobs, a bit of pressing and so on, and
then I sat down for half an hour's read, while the guests were
changing, until the dinner bugle sounded at 8.30.   I then
proceeded to my duty of tidying cabins.   C. suite, that is Mr
Blane's, being nearest, I meant to start on him but I found the
door of the drawing room locked, so I just unlocked the door with
my master key and went straight into the room.

The first thing I saw was a note addressed "Nicholas
Stodart Esq." and marked "URGENT" in capital letters. I thought
that a bit funny as if Mr. Blane had gone up to dinner why

couldn't he have taken it up to Mr. Stodart himself?   But it's
not for me to question the why and wherefores of the guests, so I
took it up to Mr. Stodart right away.

He just thanked me and tore it open.   Then, as I was
leaving the lounge to go below, he came hurrying after me and
said, "I am afraid something's wrong steward."

We went down to the late lamented's cabin together and had a
quick look round.   He wasn't in the suite and the drawing room
window was open.   Mr. Stodart told me that he was afraid the poor
gentleman had chucked himself overboard, then I spotted a bit of
paper on the writing table and gave it to Mr. Stodart saying,
"What's this here?"

He gave it a glance and sent me up to get Mr. Rocksavage
immediately.

I did as I was bid and the owner sent me for the Captain.

DETECTIVE OFFICER KETTERING'S REPORT, CONTINUED.

Having taken statements from Captain Derringham, Mr.
Rocksavage, Mr. Stodart and the cabin steward, Ringbottom, I then
proceeded to suite C. which had been allotted to Bolitho Blane.
It consisted of a drawing room, a state room and private bathroom.
On the other side of the drawing room there was a single state
room, which, I am told, had been allotted to Stodart in order that
he might be near his employer.

A cursory examination of the suite showed nothing which
called for special remark.   Captain Derringham told me that he

had had it locked up at 8.45 before ordering the ship back to Miami, so that nothing in it had been touched or disturbed since the steward, Ringbottom, discovered Blane to be missing.

I instructed Station Photographer Southwold to take the necessary shots of the suite and decided to postpone a detailed examination until morning.   Soon after arriving on board I told Police Surgeon Jacket that, as the case was one of 'man overboard,' his presence was no longer required.

At 12.50 Station Photographer Southwold had completed his work, upon which I had suite C. relocked and placed Officer Gurdon on guard outside it.   After which I went above and spoke to Captain Derringham and Mr. Rocksavage.   I told the latter that I did not think any useful purpose could be served by keeping his guests out of their beds longer, but that as a formality I should have to question them in the morning, so none of them is to be allowed ashore without permission.

In my view, at the moment, this looks like a plain case of suicide by a man in a financial jam.   Blane's innuendoes that Rocksavage intended to do him in are discounted by the statements of the secretary, Stodart, who appears convinced that for some days past Blane was not of sound mind and suffering from a form of persecution mania.

Captain Derringham seems a fine straight-forward, if rather silent, fellow and certainly not the man to permit any monkey-business upon a ship commanded by him.

Rocksavage's manner is normal and he appears surprised and

upset at the tragedy, although it should be noticed that he stated that this was only a pleasure trip, whereas it is made abundantly clear from Stodart's statement that its real objective was to cover a big business conference between Rocksavage and Blane.

On the face of it, all the guests are apparently respectable people of some social standing, and Captain Derringham gives me his assurance that no new men have been brought on in the crew this trip, or employees of Rocksavage, for any special purpose.

Apart, therefore, from Blane's innuendoes there is no evidence at all to support any suggestion outside the known facts and, in my view, it is a plain case of suicide.

I am sending Station Photographer Southwold ashore in the yacht's launch and also Detective Officer Neame, who will deliver this report. I then propose to sleep the night on board in a spare cabin which Mr. Rocksavage has placed at my disposal. Please instruct the coastguard stations to keep a look-out for the body in the unlikely event of its being washed ashore.

Keys Kettering

Detective Officer

Florida Police.

1.15 a.m.   9.3.36.   on S.Y. Golden Gull.

POLICE HEADQUARTERS,

MIAMI,

FLA.

5.20 a.m.   9.3.36.

MEMO.

To Detective Officer Kettering.

First report on Bolitho Blane received. I note your
view that there are no suspicious circumstances attached to
the case. I agree that Blane's inuendos against Rocksavage
are apparently quite unfounded and due only to Blane's
abnormal state of mind just before taking his own life.

Prints of the photographs taken by Southwold have just
come to hand and are attached herewith. In print B. you
will note two parallel lines across the carpet, running in a
curve from the table to the porthole in the drawing room.
Please make a close examination of these at once.

If, after examination of Blane's suite, you are
satisfied that no circumstances point to his death having
been framed you can give the occupants of the yacht a clear
bill, but the Captain, Rocksavage, Stodart and the steward,
Ringbottom, should be warned that they will be required to
give evidence at the inquest.

John Milton Schwab

Lieutenant, Florida Police.

*Sorry to get you out of bed so early but if the marks
on the carpet do mean any thing you'll be in time to
take special measures before the party are up and
about   J.M.S.*

'A'. BOLITHO BLANE'S DRAWING ROOM. 'C.' SUITE. AS LOCKED 8.3.36.

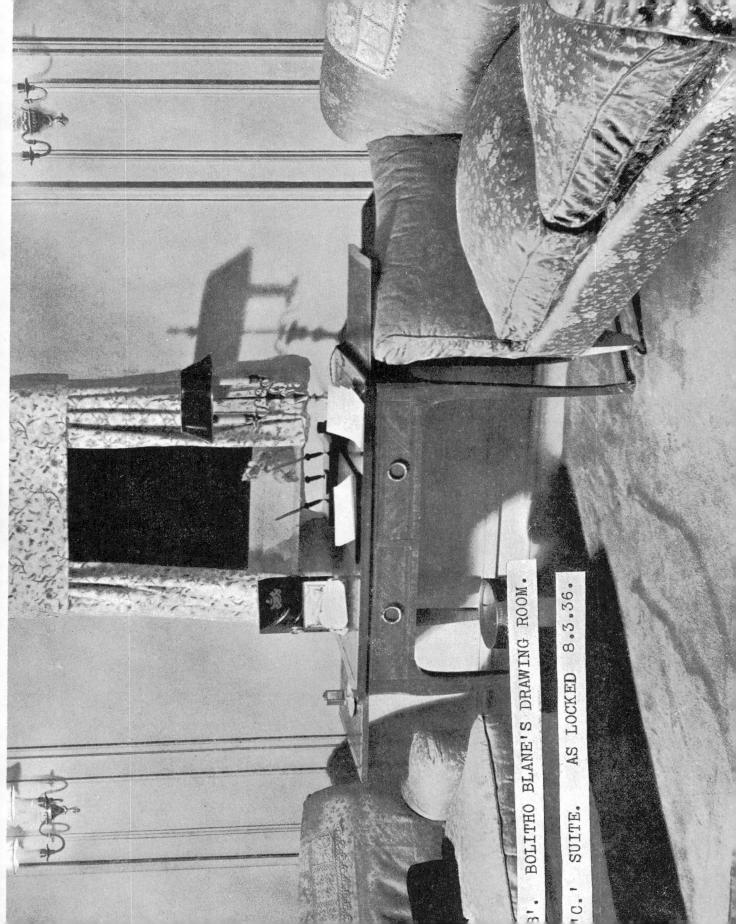

BOLITHO BLANE'S DRAWING ROOM.

SUITE. AS LOCKED 8.3.36.

'D'. BOLITHO BLANE'S BATH ROOM. 'C' SUITE. AS LOCKED 8.3.36.

'E'. NICHOLAS STODART'S STATE ROOM. AS LOCKED 8.3.36.

DETECTIVE OFFICER KETTERING'S SECOND REPORT.

On receipt of Lieutenant Schwab's memo and the photographs of C. suite on S.Y. Golden Gull I at once proceeded below in the company of Detective Officer Neame to make a thorough examination of Blane's suite in daylight.

I first examined the marks on the carpet, mentioned in Lieutenant Schwab's report, and apparent in print B.   These marks consist of a slight irregular roughing of the pile in the carpet running from the table to near the window.   Owing to the light they are not observable from the inboard side of the cabin, but only from the outboard side, which explains my failure to notice them last night, and the fact that, while appearing in print B., they are not observable in print A.

These marks might have been made by the two legs of a chair being dragged across the carpet.   I found, however, at the table end of these roughly parallel tracks a very slightly discoloured patch upon the carpet, which would not have been visible in electric light.

I then proceeded to examine the porthole window and found upon the left hand curtain a smear of blood.

Returning to the patch on the carpet it seemed to me probable that a small quantity of blood had been spilled here too and that someone had endeavoured to get it out by rubbing the place with a wet sponge.

If the person had done this immediately after the blood was spilled, as is probable, most of the blood would have been

absorbed, hence the faintness of the discolouration.   The patch
is still damp and measures about eight inches by five, although it
is probable that, if the blood was spilled here, it was no more
than a few drops and the main patch of damp was caused by an
endeavour to clean the carpet afterwards.

In view of this, the tracks on the carpet present a new
significance, and I suggest that they were caused by the toes of a
man's boots as he was dragged from the table to the porthole.

Taken in conjunction the wet patch, the boot tracks, and the
smear of blood upon the window curtain definitely point to the
fact that Bolitho Blane was murdered.

I send this report at once in order that full investigation
may be made into the antecedents of all the passengers upon the
yacht, who now come under suspicion.

I have given instructions that, as they leave their cabins
for breakfast, each cabin is to be locked after them.   I shall
then be able to search all cabins before these are tidied and will
proceed to the examination of all parties concerned immediately
they have breakfasted.

Korp Kettering

Detective Officer
Florida Police.

7.35 a.m.   9.3.36.   on S.Y. Golden Gull.

Police Department.
Form RL/2120/C.7.

SECTION OF CURTAIN REMOVED FROM LEFT HAND SIDE OF BOLITHO BLANE'S

CABIN WINDOW AT 6.45 a.m.   9.3.36.

Police Department.
Form RL/2120/C.7.

DETECTIVE OFFICER KETTERING'S THIRD REPORT.

The guests, with the exception of Lady Welter and the Bishop of Bude, who breakfasted in their respective cabins, assembled for breakfast in the dining saloon between 8.50 and 9.25. As each of them left their cabins these were locked after them and the keys brought to me.

They had finished breakfast by 9.50, so I took over a small writing room and proceeded to the examination of all parties, first recalling Mr. Rocksavage.

Police Department.
Form RL/2120/C.7.

DETECTIVE OFFICER NEAME'S SHORTHAND NOTES OF DETECTIVE OFFICER
KETTERING'S EXAMINATION OF MR. CARLTON ROCKSAVAGE.

K.   Come in Mr. Rocksavage, come in. I am sorry to upset your
trip like this but there are just one or two little things I have
got to ask, so that we can clear this matter up.   I hope it
didn't give you a bad night.

R.   No, thank you.   I slept perfectly well.   Naturally I was a
bit upset at anything like this happening on my yacht and it was a
shock for my guests, too, but it wasn't as if Bolitho Blane was a
personal friend of mine.   As I had never met the man any distress
I have been feeling is more general than particular.

K.   Sure, sure.   Of course it's not like losing a personal
friend.   I quite see that.   Now, Mr. Rocksavage, I want you to
tell me the real reason for this trip.

R.   As I said last night, it's merely a pleasure jaunt, to get a
little sunbathing and big-game fishing with a few friends.

K.   Mr. Bolitho Blane was not a friend of yours, so you say.

R.   Well, it's true I'd never met him, but we corresponded a lot
and we happen to be in the same line of business, so I figured
this was a good opportunity to make his acquaintance.

K.   Business.   Now we're getting somewhere I think.   Just what
was the business you proposed to transact with Blane on this trip?

R.   It was a pleasure party I tell you.

K.   Now, Mr. Rocksavage, that won't do.   I had a talk with Mr.
Stodart last night and he seems to have known quite a bit about
Blane's affairs, so I think you'd best be open with me.

R.   I see.   Stodart let out the fact that Blane and I meant to do a deal if it were possible, did he?   Well, that's true.

K.   That's better now.   Why didn't you let me in on that the first time?

R.   Well, this is a quite unforeseen and very unfortunate affair.   I am sure you will understand that the last thing I want is any undue publicity.

K.   Sure, sure.

R.   As you may know, I'm president of Rocksavage Consolidated, and the man behind its associated companies, which between them control the biggest share of the soap output in the world.

It is common knowledge, too, that Bolitho Blane was the big man of the British group, who are our principal competitors.   A price war, ruinous to both parties, has been going on for years and I considered that the best thing to do was for Blane and me to get together, see if we couldn't arrange some sort of an amalgamation, and put our concerns on a more solid footing.

If anyone had come to know what was in the air the shares of both groups would have gone up like a sky rocket, and neither Blane nor I wanted that.   It would have meant such a terrible slump afterwards if we'd failed to make a deal.   You'll see, then, it was essential we should meet some place where nobody would get to know about it.   I suggested my yacht, and Blane agreed.   He was to have joined us before we left New York by sea plane, but he sent a message at the last moment saying that he couldn't make it, and would come aboard at Miami.

He came off in a tender just before 7 o'clock last evening and went straight down to his cabin.   I have already told you what occurred after that.

K.   Thanks Mr. Rocksavage.   That's fine.   I can quite understand your not wishing your intended conference with Mr. Blane to get about, owing to its effect on the market.   Now, tell me about these other guests of yours.   Was it in any sense a pleasure trip, or were all of them concerned in this business with you and Blane?

R.   One or two were here on account of business.

K.   Which were they?

R.   Lady Welter.   You'll have heard of her, I expect.   She's the widow of the shipping man, Sir David Welter, who made a big pile in the war.   He died soon after, but his widow's a wonderful business woman as well, although in many ways she's much more concerned with politics and social good.   She runs a group of papers in Great Britain and they cost her a tidy packet I believe, but that's her business.   She has an outsize income and so she can afford it.   A lot of her money is tied up in my companies.   In fact, she is my biggest individual shareholder and I value her opinion, so that's why I asked her to join us for this trip. She's an old friend of mine though and, quite outside any business operations, she's been my guest on this yacht and other places, many times before this.

K.   Anyone else?

R.   Well, I suppose you'd include young Reggie Jocelyn.   He's

her son-in-law, and the old lady thinks a lot of him.   Since he
married the daughter she runs him around and asks his opinion on
most things that she does.

K.   And the Jap?

R.   Yes, he's business, too.   I've never met him before
yesterday, although we've corresponded.

K.   What part does he play?

R.   Well, he's a sort of unofficial representative of the
Japanese government, and he's been playing ball with me for some
time now on the proposition of our securing a monopoly of the
Japanese market for our goods.   He was playing ball with Blane,
too, I don't doubt, anyhow neither of us had seen our way to close
the deal up to date but I figured that, if Blane and I could get
together, we'd have the Jap cold between us so we both postponed
clinching matters until we'd had our talk.   I asked the Jap along
so that, if we settled things satisfactorily, we could tackle him
together afterwards, and kill two birds at one sitting.

K.   How about the others.

R.   They're just straight-forward guests who know nothing of the
business which Blane and I were proposing to transact.

K.   Thank you Mr. Rocksavage.   That makes the situation a whole
lot clearer.   I am afraid no one must go ashore yet, but I'll be
seeing you when I've had a chat with these other people.

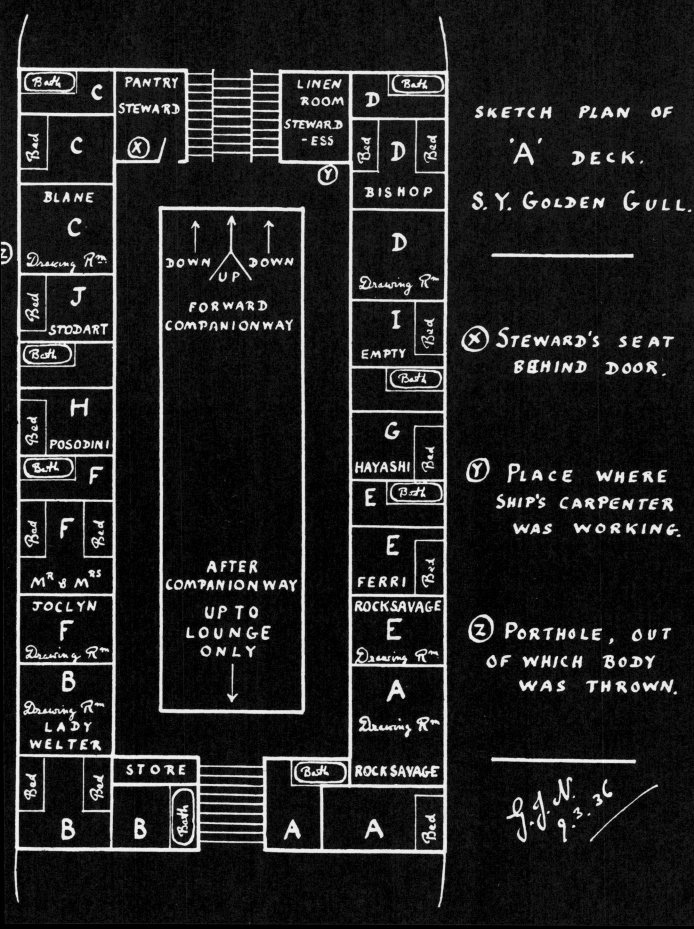

SKETCH PLAN OF
'A' DECK.
S.Y. GOLDEN GULL.

Ⓧ STEWARD'S SEAT
BEHIND DOOR.

Ⓨ PLACE WHERE
SHIP'S CARPENTER
WAS WORKING.

Ⓩ PORTHOLE, OUT
OF WHICH BODY
WAS THROWN.

G.J.N.
9.3.36

DETECTIVE OFFICER NEAME'S SHORTHAND NOTES OF DETECTIVE OFFICER

KETTERING'S EXAMINATION OF CABIN STEWARD, SILAS RINGBOTTOM.

K.   'Morning Ringbottom.

R.   Good morning, sir.

K.   Have you been on board this ship long?

R.   Yes sir; ever since Mr. Rocksavage bought her, and before

that, too, with the previous owner, Lord Foulkes.   I am an

ex-navy man and this was my first job on leaving the service.

K.   Good.   Well, there are just one or two things I want to ask

you about this affair that occurred last night.   According to

what you told me then, after you had been to Mr. Blane's suite to

enquire if he wanted you to unpack, you went straight back to your

pantry, did a few odd jobs there, and then read a book until the

dinner bugle sounded.   Now, is that correct?

R.   Yes sir, that's correct.

K.   You're quite sure you never left that pantry of yours?   I'm

not trying to pin anything on you, don't think that, but I want

you to be quite certain that you're not making any mistakes.

R.   Wait a minute, sir: I did leave it just once, to slip up to

the writing room to get some sheets of notepaper for the Japanese

gentleman.   He'd asked for it earlier on, but I found the racks

were empty and, as the chief steward had been ashore at Miami, the

store room was locked.   When the Jap rang for me again later,

though, the chief steward was back again in his cabin and he gave

me some from the store.

K.   What time was that?

R.   A bit before eight bells sir.

K.   Just before eight o'clock, eh?   And, apart from that, you never left your pantry?

R.   No, that's the truth sir.

K.   Who else was on duty at that time?

R.   Only me sir.   The other stewards who help with the cabins was at their job of laying up for dinner then; and the stewardess, Maud Briggs, what would have been on duty, went down with shingles two days ago, so she's in the sick bay.   Fortunately there's only three ladies aboard, and two of them has their own maids, so they're looking after the other lady between them.

K.   Can you bring anybody to prove that you were in your pantry during all that time?

R.   Well, may be it's lucky for me sir.   In the ordinary way I wouldn't be able to, the stewardess being ill, but, as it happens, I can.   Syd Jenks, the ship's carpenter, was doing a job of work in the passage way during the whole of that time and we passed the time of day, as you may say, quite frequent, while he was at it. He knows I never left my pantry, except to get the Jap his notepaper, not before the dinner bugle went.

K.   Did it strike you as unusual that Mr. Blane's cabin door was locked when you went to tidy it up?

R.   No sir, not particular.   Visitors varies, some's open handed, some's not.   Some's suspicious, some's not.   Visitors who haven't sailed with us before sometimes locks their cabin doors for the first day or two out, then they don't bother no more.   I didn't think nothing of it.   I just unlocked the door with my master key and went straight into the room.

K.   That's good.   Now, from your pantry you can't see the door of Mr. Blane's suite, can you?

R.   No sir.   You see my pantry's an inside cabin, so I can't see round the corner along the passage way.

K.   No.   That's quite obvious from the ship's plans I've got in front of me.   So you wouldn't be able to see if anyone approached Mr. Blane's cabin from the lounge, would you?

R.   No sir.

K.   But you would be able to see anybody who came the other way, from the forward companion-way, which leads to the upper and lower decks, wouldn't you?

R.   I would that sir.

K.   Was your pantry door open during this time?

R.   Yes sir.

K.   Now, think carefully, Ringbottom.   Did you see any member of the crew, or any other person, come either up or down the companion-way and pass your door, going in the direction of Mr. Blane's cabin between 7.45 and 8.30 last night?

R.   Only Miss Rocksavage's maid sir, going along to dress her, no one else.

K.   But you would have, if they had?

R.   Yes sir.   I couldn't have helped seeing them.

K.   Right.   That's all I wanted to know.

DETECTIVE OFFICER NEAME'S SHORTHAND NOTES OF DETECTIVE OFFICER KETTERING'S EXAMINATION OF SYD JENKS, SHIP'S CARPENTER.

K.   Good morning Jenks.

J.   Good morning sir.

K.   How long have you been on board this ship?

J.   Just on two years sir. Ever since Captain Derringham took over. He brought me with him from his previous ship, the Southern Cross.

K.   Right. Now, d'you mind telling me where you were between 7.30 and 8.30 last night.

J.   I was fitting new skirting boards to the stewardess's pantry on A. deck from just before 7.30 sir.

K.   From where you were working could you see the door of Mr. Blane's suite?

J.   No sir. I was working on the starboard side, just across from the for'ard companion-way.

K.   Was the companion-way in your view the whole time?

J.   Yes sir.

K.   Did you see anyone go up or down it during the time you were working there?

J.   Lady Welter's maid went below just after I set to work.

K.   Just after 7.30, eh?

J.   Yes sir. Then Nellie Orde, Miss Rocksavage's maid, came up to dress her mistress much later on, about ten past eight I should say.

K.   Anyone else?

J.   No sir.

K.   Could you see the entrance of the steward's pantry from where you were?

J.   Yes sir.   It was just across the companion-way on the portside.

K.   Was anyone there, d'you know?

J.   Yes sir.   The cabin steward, Mr. Ringbottom.

K.   Was he in his pantry the whole time you were at your job?

J.   Yes sir, except when he went to answer the Japanese gentle-man's bell, and then off to the chief steward to get some note-paper from him out of the store.   He remarked, I remember, about the slackness of the lounge steward in letting it run out in the writing room because someone else had asked for some earlier on in the afternoon, when the chief steward was ashore, and there wasn't none.

K.   What time was that?

J.   I'm afraid I couldn't say sir.

K.   Can you give me any idea.

J.   I'd hardly like to say the time, you see I didn't notice partic'lar, being busy on my job.

K.   Was it before, or after, eight?

J.   Oh, before eight.   Maybe about a quarter to, but I wouldn't like to say for certain.   Ringbottom was away about five minutes then, but all the rest of the time he was in his pantry because, although we couldn't see each other, every now and then we exchanged remarks.

K.   Did you see anybody else in the passage-way during the time you were working there?

J.   Only the Bishop sir, when he went up.   That was at eight o'clock, because I heard the ship's bell strike immediately after.

K.   But various other people must have been coming down from the lounge or going back up to it, during that time.

J.   That's true, of course, but the companion-way to the lounge is way aft, nowhere near where I was.   I heard cabin doors shutting now and then, but you see I had my back to the passage-way most of the time and I didn't take much notice what happened behind me, being busy with my job.

K.   What time did you stop work ?

J.   Just after the dinner bugle sounded at 8.30.

K.   Right.   That's all I want to know.   Thank you, Jenks.

J.   You're welcome sir.

FERRI ROCKSAVAGE.   RETAKE FROM PHOTOGRAPH IN FATHER'S CABIN.   9.3.36.

<u>DETECTIVE OFFICER NEAME'S SHORTHAND NOTES OF DETECTIVE OFFICER</u>

<u>KETTERING'S EXAMINATION OF MISS FERRI ROCKSAVAGE.</u>

K.   Good morning Miss Rocksavage.   Come right in.

F.R.   Good morning.

K.   Come and sit down.   There are just a few questions I want
to ask you about this unfortunate business last night.

F.R.   Certainly; anything I can do ....

K.   Would you just tell me, Miss Rocksavage, what you were
doing, and where you were, from the time the yacht sailed until
you went in to dinner.

F.R.   When the ship left Miami I was sitting on the port deck with
Mr. Jocelyn.

K.   Did you see Mr. Blane come aboard?

F.R.   No.   We were on the port side of the ship: that is, we
were facing out to sea.   We sat there until about 7.15, and then
we both went below to our cabins.   I got interested in a book, so
I was a little late in changing and I didn't get up to the lounge
until about 8.40.   The other guests were all there, except Mr.
Bolitho Blane and his secretary, neither of whom I had met, and I
was just looking round for my father when the steward came up with
a message from him.   He said to me, "Mr. Rocksavage says, Miss,
would you please take everybody in to dinner.   Mr. Blane has had
a heart attack, so we are returning to Miami."

K.   And what happened then?

F.R.   I did as my father had asked me to and I didn't know
anything about what really happened until father told us all after

we had anchored off Miami again; just a few minutes before the police came on board.

K.   Did you know of any special reason for this trip?

F.R.   No.

K.   Are you certain of that?

F.R.   Well, it's just a pleasure trip, like lots of others we've had on the yacht, but as there were several strangers on board I naturally assumed that some big business deal would be discussed during the time we were at sea. Father often uses these trips to entertain people with whom, if he were seen ashore, comment might be aroused which would affect the markets.

K.   I see.   Thank you, Miss Rocksavage.   That'll be all for the moment.

HON. R. JOCELYN.   RETAKE FROM PHOTOGRAPH IN LADY WELTER'S CABIN.   9.3.36.

DETECTIVE OFFICER NEAME'S SHORTHAND NOTES OF DETECTIVE OFFICER
KETTERING'S EXAMINATION OF THE HONOURABLE REGINALD JOCELYN.

K.   Good morning, Mr. Jocelyn.   Now, I'd just like you to tell
me anything you can about this unfortunate affair last night.

J.   I'm afraid I can't tell you anything.

K.   Well, let's hear what you were doing between the time of the
ship's sailing and your going in to dinner.

J.   When the ship sailed I was sitting on deck with Miss
Rocksavage.   We stayed there until the ship was well out to sea
and somewhere about 7.30 we went down to our cabins to change for
dinner.   I came up to the lounge at 8.30 and Mr. Rocksavage
arrived soon after.   A steward spoke to him and he went below,
then a message came up that Mr. Blane was ill, so we were
returning to Miami.   After that we went in to dinner.

K.   Do you always take an hour to change your clothes?

J.   Sometimes an hour, and sometimes two if I feel like it.

K.   No need to get fresh now.   Were you changing all that time?

J.   I don't see what the devil it's got to do with you but, if
you must know, I spent a long time lying in my bath.

K.   Thanks.   Now, this trip.   You were in on the object of it,
weren't you?

J.   I don't understand what you mean.

K.   Oh, yes you do.   Bolitho Blane and Carlton Rocksavage were
using this as a meeting ground to patch up a truce in the
commercial war they've been waging.

J.   Oh; that.   Yes.

K.   That, yes!   And how much more did you know about it?

J.   Nothing, except that Lady Welter, my mother-in-law, has very large holdings in the Rocksavage companies, and that she always likes me to stand by so that I can advise her where her business interests are concerned.

K.   Right.   That'll do for the moment, Mr. Jocelyn.

PAMELA JOCELYN.   RETAKE FROM PHOTOGRAPH IN LADY WELTER'S CABIN.   9.3.36.

DETECTIVE OFFICER NEAME'S SHORTHAND NOTES OF DETECTIVE OFFICER

KETTERING'S EXAMINATION OF THE HONOURABLE MRS. REGINALD JOCELYN.

K.   Good morning, Mrs. Jocelyn.   Sit down, won't you?

P.J.   Thank you.

K.   Now, just what can you tell me about this unfortunate affair

last night?

P.J.   Nothing at all, I'm afraid.

K.   It would help me to check up on things if you wouldn't mind

giving me your movements from the time the ship sailed until you

went in to dinner.

P.J.   I am afraid that's not going to help you much and, after

all, it's quite clear that this Mr. Blane took his own life, isn't it?

K.   Sure - sure, Mrs. Jocelyn.   It's only a matter of routine

procedure that I have to bother everybody like this.   Just where

did you happen to be when the yacht left Miami?

P.J.   I was in the lounge with Count Posodini.

K.   Anyone else there?

P.J.   No, not until Mr. Rocksavage arrived.

K.   What happened then?

P.J.   We had more drinks and talked for a bit, then Mr. Blane's

secretary came in and was introduced to us.   There was some talk

about his sending a message down to Mr. Blane, and just after that

I said that I must go down and change for dinner.   Count Posodini

said that he thought he would, too, so we went below together.

K.   What time would that be?

P.J.   About ten minutes to eight.

K.   And then?

P.J.   I changed and came up to the lounge with my husband again just as the dinner bugle sounded at 8.30.   A few minutes later a steward came in and spoke to Mr. Rocksavage, who had just come in, and they both went below together.

K.   Yes, go on please.

P.J.   I was talking to my mother when a message came up from Mr. Rocksavage that Mr. Blane had had some sort of an attack, and so we were returning to Miami.   Ferri Rocksavage said that we had better go in to dinner without her father, so in we went.

K.   Just when did you know the real cause of the trouble?

P.J.   Not until the yacht was anchored off Miami again.   Mr. Rocksavage told us then, and said that the police would be coming on board in a few moments.

K.   Good.   Now, did you regard this just as a pleasure trip?

P.J.   Not altogether.   I know that my mother has a big interest in the Rocksavage companies and, as Bolitho Blane was expected to join us at Miami, I thought that there must be something in the wind.   Anyone would, who knew that Blane and Rocksavage were the two soap kings, but I wasn't particularly interested, because it's not really anything to do with me.

K.   Your husband advises your mother, though, where her financial interests are concerned, doesn't he?

P.J.   Yes, but we go about with mother quite a lot on social parties, where no business comes under discussion at all.

K.   Thank you, Mrs. Jocelyn, that'll do for the present.

LADY WELTER.

RETAKE FROM PHOTOGRAPH IN HER DAUGHTER'S CABIN. 9.3.36.

DETECTIVE OFFICER NEAME'S SHORTHAND NOTES OF DETECTIVE OFFICER KETTERING'S EXAMINATION OF LADY WELTER.

K.   Good morning, Lady Welter.   Take a chair, please.

L.W.   Thank you, I prefer to stand.

K.   Just as you wish, lady.

L.W.   What is it you wish to see me about?

K.   Isn't that rather obvious?   You know that I'm the officer in charge of the investigation of Mr. Bolitho Blane's death.

L.W.   And what has that to do with me?

K.   Nothing - nothing, as far as I know, Lady Welter, but this is just a matter of routine and you won't mind answering a few questions, I'm sure.

L.W.   That all depends on the questions, young man.

K.   Well, they're quite simple.   It's just a matter of routine checking up, and I'd like you to tell me just what your movements were between the time of the yacht sailing from Miami and your going in to dinner last night.

L.W.   Are you accusing me ....

K.   Now, now, have a heart, please.   I'm not accusing anyone of anything, but it's my duty to get all these details which may seem stupid to you.   Where were you when the ship sailed?

L.W.   I was on deck talking to the Bishop of Bude.

K.   Whereabouts on deck?

L.W.   By the rail.   I was leaning on it, if you must know.

K.   Yes, but in what part of the ship?

L.W.   I was facing the land.

K.   You saw the tender come off then?

L.W.   I did and the Bishop said to me, "That's Mr. Bolitho Blane," as the two men came up the gangway in to the middle of the ship.

K.   The Bishop knew Blane by sight, then?

L.W.   I don't know.   I suppose so.

K.   Right, what happened after that?

L.W.   The Bishop and I went down to our cabins.   When I came up to the lounge I found Mr. Rocksavage with Mr. Blane's secretary and the Bishop.   The secretary was introduced to me and we sat there until Mr. Rocksavage left.

K.   What time was that?

L.W.   I really haven't the faintest idea.   What has all this to do ....

K.   Patience, please.   What happened after Mr. Rocksavage left the lounge?

L.W.   If you must know, the Japanese gentleman came in and then my daughter and son-in-law, Mr. and Mrs. Jocelyn.   After the dinner bugle sounded Mr. Rocksavage came in, too, but he went downstairs almost at once and some message came up that Mr. Blane was ill, so that we were to go in to dinner without waiting any longer.

K.   Am I right in believing that you hold a large block of shares in the Rocksavage companies?

L.W.   That, young man, is nothing whatsoever to do with you.

K.   Did you come on this trip for pleasure?

L.W.   For my own reasons.   This discussion is quite pointless.

K.   All right, all right.   I won't trouble you any more now, Lady Welter, but maybe we'll have to have one of these jolly little discussions together again, a little later on.

ISHOP OF BUDE.   RETAKE FROM PHOTOGRAPH IN LADY WELTER'S CABIN.   9.3.36.

DETECTIVE OFFICER NEAME'S SHORTHAND NOTES OF DETECTIVE OFFICER KETTERING'S EXAMINATION OF THE VERY REVEREND DR. STAPLETON THOMAS, D.D., THE LORD BISHOP OF BUDE.

K.   Good morning, Bishop.

B.   Good morning - good morning.   This is a very distressing affair - very distressing.

K.   It certainly is, and I am sure you will forgive me bothering you, but I have got to ask you just a few questions, so that I can check up on events last night.

B.   Of course.   I am the last person to wish to obstruct you in your duties, officer.   Any information that I can give is entirely at your service.

K.   That's nice of you, Bishop.   I only wish that all the people I've had to question looked on things like that.   Now, perhaps you'll just tell me what you were doing between the time of the ship sailing and going in to dinner last night.

B.   I was standing by the after-rail on the starboard side of the ship, with Lady Welter, when we left Miami.

K.   You saw Blane and his secretary come aboard, then?

B.   Yes.

K.   You are quite certain that it was Blane?

B.   Oh, yes.   I remarked to Lady Welter at the time how very much older he was looking.

K.   You knew him before then?

B.   I would hardly say that I knew him, but we met once about seven years ago.   He was staying in an English country house where I also chanced to be a guest.

K.   What happened after that?

B.   Lady Welter and I went below shortly after the ship sailed.
I changed for dinner and came up to the lounge at 8 o'clock.   I
can state the time with certainty as the ship's bell was sounded
just as I went up the companion-way.   My host, Mr. Rocksavage,
was there with Mr. Stodart.   A few minutes after that Lady Welter
came in and then Mr. Rocksavage went below to change, remarking
as he did so that he had left it very late and, if he were not up
on time, we were to go in to dinner without him.

     Lady Welter and I talked with Mr. Stodart for a time, and
then a Japanese gentleman, who had come aboard in the afternoon,
joined us.   Mr. and Mrs. Jocelyn came in next - no, no, I'm wrong
there - Count Posodini arrived after the Japanese, then the
Jocelyns, just before the dinner bugle sounded.

     Mr. Rocksavage was a little late and had no sooner arrived
in the lounge than he was sent for to go below.   We stood about
for a few minutes, and then Miss Rocksavage came in.   Soon after
she received a message from her father that Mr. Blane had been
taken ill, so that the yacht was returning to Miami, and that we
were to go in to dinner without waiting any longer.

K.   Thanks, Bishop.   That's all nice and clear.   Now, what can
you tell me about the objects of this party?

B.   Well, it's just a pleasure trip, you know.   I had hoped
that it would be a most pleasant relaxation from my arduous
duties.   I have a large flock you know - a large flock.

K.   But you were aware, surely, that Lady Welter is a very rich woman and a considerable portion of her fortune is invested in the Rocksavage companies?

B.   Yes, I was aware of that.   Lady Welter is a very old friend of mine - one of my oldest and, you will not misunderstand me when I say, one of my dearest friends.   Those papers that she controls at home wield an enormous influence for good, and it has been my privilege on many occasions to advise her on questions of policy for those papers.

K.   She might well have consulted you then if the money which supports those papers was in jeopardy?

B.   Yes, she certainly might have done so as an old friend, you know - a very old friend.

K.   But you didn't actually know that this trip was cover for a big business deal in which Rocksavage, Bolitho Blane and Lady Welter were concerned?

B.   No.   I was not actually aware of that.

K.   And, although you had known Blane previously, you did not have any communication with him while he was on board this ship?

(AT THIS POINT STODART, WHOM WE HAD SENT FOR EARLIER FOR THE PURPOSE OF GETTING A FLASH PHOTOGRAPH OF HIM, CAME INTO THE CABIN.   I SNAPPED HIM AS HE ENTERED.   WE THEN SAW THAT THE BISHOP HAD COLLAPSED IN HIS CHAIR.   AFTER A MOMENT HE CAME ROUND OUT OF HIS FAINT, APOLOGISED AND MENTIONED THAT HE HAD HAD NO BREAKFAST, ALSO THAT HE SUFFERED FROM HIS HEART.   DETECTIVE OFFICER KETTERING, HAVING CONCLUDED HIS EXAMINATION, HE ALLOWED THE BISHOP TO WITHDRAW IN STODART'S COMPANY.)

NOSUKE HAYASHI.   FLASHED BY DETECTIVE OFFICER NEAME.   9.3.36.

Police Department,
Form RL/2120/C.7.

<u>DETECTIVE OFFICER NEAME'S SHORTHAND NOTES OF DETECTIVE OFFICER</u>

<u>KETTERING'S EXAMINATION OF MR. INOSUKE HAYASHI.</u>

K.   Good morning Mr. Hayashi.   Just sit down and answer a few questions, will you?

H.   Certainly.

K.   Will you give me your movements please from the time you came on board this yacht until you went in to dinner last night.

H.   Oh yes.   I came on board from a launch at 4.30 yesterday afternoon.   After visiting my cabin I had tea with my host and some of the other guests.   About ten past six I went down to my cabin again to do some work, and remained there until after I had changed for dinner.

At 8.15 I came into the lounge, where I found the Bishop and Lady Welter, whom I had met at tea.   The latter introduced me to Mr. Stodart whom I had not seen before.

(FROM THIS POINT INOSUKE HAYASHI'S STATEMENT CONFIRMS THAT OF THE OTHERS.)

K.   Now, I'd like to know the reason for your coming on this trip.

H.   At the invitation of Mr. Rocksavage.   We are business friends - it is nice to meet each other - and enjoy the pleasures of such excellent company upon his very beautiful yacht.

K.   Now, that won't do, and the sooner you come clean with me the better.   This pleasure trip was a blind to cover a big business deal between Rocksavage and Blane.   You're going to tell me just what part you were going to play in that.

H.   I tell you anything you like.   When I say that it is a pleasure trip I speak truthfully, but I have already said that I was a business friend of Mr. Rocksavage, too.   When business men are together, even for pleasure, their conversation is of their business also, most of the time, as I have frequently observed.

K.   You knew, then, that business would come under discussion?

H.   Certainly I knew that.

K.   Well, let's hear the part you were going to play in it.

H.   I have the honour to act for the Shikoku Products Company, which is associated with my government.   Shikoku handles various commercial concessions for the Ministry of the Interior and one of these has to do with the supply of soap to the armed forces and also civil services of Japan.   This monopoly is of considerable value and Shikoku hoped to raise a loan of ten to twelve million dollars on it.   Also, this monopoly would have considerable value for whatever company acquired it since, if they wished, they could float a subsidiary company upon the prospective profits which the monopoly will bring and thus attract considerable new public money to their business.

K.   And you were about to sell this monopoly to either Rocksavage or Blane?

H.   That is so.   I have been negotiating by correspondence with both for some time.   A fortnight ago, however, Mr. Rocksavage cabled me that negotiations could go no further until after a conference he proposed to hold on this date.   He suggested that I should join the party and said that, if I did so, he had every reason to believe that the affair might be concluded to the

satisfaction of all concerned.   I sailed from San Francisco to

Panama and from there I came overland to join his yacht at Miami.

K.   I see.   That will do.

UNT LUIGI POSODINI.　　FLASHED BY DETECTIVE OFFICER NEAME.　　9.3.36.

Police Department.
Form RL/2120/C.7.

DETECTIVE OFFICER NEAME'S SHORTHAND NOTES OF DETECTIVE OFFICER KETTERING'S EXAMINATION OF COUNT POSODINI.

P.   Hello! Hello! Has this writing room been converted into a photographic studio overnight?

K.   No. Come in, Count. It's just that we're taking a flash of all the guests on board before we examine them. Matter of routine, that's all. Sit down, will you ? There are just a few questions I'd like to ask you about this unfortunate affair last night.

P.   Fire away, friend, fire away!

K.   From your name I had imagined you to be an Italian, but you talk like an American.

P.   I am an Italian, but I have lived in the States nearly all my life. My mother was an American and she had the money so, although I still have the old place in Italy, I regard New York as home.

K.   I see. Now, would you mind telling me what your movements were from the time the yacht sailed till you went in to dinner last night.

P.   There's no mystery about that. I was having a drink in the lounge with Mrs. Jocelyn when the engines started to turn over. A few moments later Mr. Rocksavage joined us. We had another spot with him and then Blane's secretary, a chap called Stodart, came in and made himself known to us. We had another round of drinks to keep him company while he was taking some notes of share prices off the board for his boss. The lounge steward took those down to Blane's cabin for him and came up to say that he couldn't get any answer to his knock, so Stodart told him to take them down again and push them under the cabin door.

Just after that I said I thought it was about time to go below and change.

K.   Can you tell me what time that would have been ?

P.   About a quarter of eight.   Mrs. Jocelyn said she thought she would go down, too, so we went down together, after which I went straight to my cabin.

I came up to the lounge again about 8.25, and when the dinner bugle sounded most of the guests were assembled there.

(FROM THIS POINT COUNT POSODINI'S STATEMENT CONFIRMS THAT OF THE OTHERS.)

K.   Now, Count, what d'you know about the real motive for this party?

P.   Real motive?   There's only one as far as I know - stealing a little summer down in these waters before New York becomes livable again.   I'm just mad about sunshine, but maybe that's my Italian blood.

K.   D'you mean to tell me you had no idea that an amalgamation between the big soap interests was to be negotiated during this trip?

P.   That's news to me.   The only thing that I know about soap is that it's useful to wash with.

K.   How long have you known Mr. Rocksavage?

P.   Just three and a half days.

K.   You'd never met him, then, before you came on board at New York?

P.   No sir.

K.   How long have you known Bolitho Blane?

P.   I'd never met him, either.   I'd heard of him, of course, as a big financier, but I didn't even know that he was interested in soap.

K.   All right.   What about the Jap, Inosuke Hayashi?   How long have you known him?

P.   The same applies.   I didn't even know of his existence before he came on board yesterday afternoon.

K.   But if you've never had any dealings with any of these people can you give me a satisfactory explanation as to why Rocksavage invited you to join this outfit?

P.   He didn't.   It was Reggie Jocelyn who asked me if I'd like to come along for a few days' sunshine and big-game fishing.

K.   How long have you known Jocelyn?

P.   I met him coming over in the Normandie, and later developed the acquaintance in New York.   His wife is Lady Welter's daughter and I gather that Lady Welter is a very old friend of Mr. Rocksavage.   In fact, although Miss Rocksavage is nominally hostess here, Lady Welter gave me the impression that she was running the party and, as the invitation came from her son-in-law, I didn't hesitate to accept it.

K.   Thank you, Count.   That'll do for the present.

Police Department.
Form RL/2120/C.7.

DETECTIVE OFFICER NEAME'S SHORTHAND NOTES OF DETECTIVE OFFICER

KETTERING'S EXAMINATION OF THE LOUNGE STEWARD, JACK CANE.

K.   Come in, Cane.   I just want to ask you a few questions about what occurred last night.

C.   Yes sir.

K.   How long have you been in the employ of Mr. Rocksavage?

C.   A year and three months sir.

K.   What were you doing before that?

C.   I was third barman at the Biltmore in New York.   I did eighteen months there and before that I was at the Sporting Club in Havana, doing lounge waiter.

K.   That's all right; now, I want you to tell me all that you can remember about which guests came and went from the lounge from the time of the ship's sailing until they went in to dinner last night.

      (CANE'S STATEMENT CONFIRMS THE TIMES OF ARRIVAL AND DEPARTURE OF THE GUESTS FROM THE LOUNGE, AS GIVEN BY THEMSELVES BETWEEN THE TIME OF SAILING AT 7.5. AND THEIR GOING IN TO DINNER AT 8.40.)

K.   Were you in the lounge the whole of that time?

C.   Yes, I was there the whole time, sir, as they kept me pretty busy mixing drinks, except, of course, for two brief absences between 7.40 and 7.45.   Mr. Stodart took down some figures from the notice board in his pocket book, tore out the leaf and asked me to take it down to Mr. Blane's cabin.   I knocked and there was no reply, so I took it up again, and then Mr. Stodart remarked that Mr. Blane was probably in his bath, so he sent me down with it again and told me to slip it under Mr. Blane's door which I did.

K.   That'll do.   You can go now.

DETECTIVE OFFICER NEAME'S SHORTHAND NOTES OF DETECTIVE OFFICER

KETTERING'S SECOND EXAMINATION OF THE HONOURABLE REGINALD JOCELYN.

K.   Sorry to bother you again Mr. Jocelyn, but I understand that

Count Posodini joined this party at your invitation.

J.   Yes, that's right.

K.   Now, what part does he play in this business deal which

Rocksavage, Blane and the Jap contemplated putting through?

J.   None at all. He doesn't know anything about it.

K.   Why did you ask him then?

J.   Because he's a nice fellow and I thought it would give the

gathering more the appearance of a pleasure trip to have someone

there who didn't know anything about the business which was

contemplated.

K.   I see.   How long have you known him?

J.   About five weeks.   I met him coming over in the Normandie.

K.   Thanks Mr. Jocelyn.   That's all for the moment.

DETECTIVE OFFICER KETTERING'S THIRD REPORT, CONTINUED.

From the foregoing statements it is obvious that, as we have a note in Blane's own hand, scribbled on the back of the leaf torn from Stodart's pocket book with the share quotations on it, which was sent down to him at 7.45, he must still have been alive at that time.

The steward, Ringbottom, entered his cabin at 8.30 and discovered him to be missing. Therefore, Bolitho Blane must have been murdered between 7.45 and 8.30. The situation of the cabin steward's pantry and Ringbottom's statement, backed by that of the carpenter, Jenks, rules out the possibility of the crime having been committed by any member of the crew and we must, therefore, assume that the guilty party is either Carlton Rocksavage or one of his guests.

After I had questioned Count Posodini, Detective Officer Neame told me that he felt certain that this man's face was familiar to him, and that we had him on our criminal records. Every effort should, therefore, be made to obtain full particulars regarding him at once.

Having taken statements from all the guests and the only members of the crew who might possibly have been concerned in the affair I proceeded to analyse their statements with a view to seeing how far they vouch for each other, and the limited time in each case, when they were on their own, during the period 7.45-8.30, during which the murder must have been committed.

TIMES ACCOUNTED FOR BY PRESENCE IN THE LOUNGE.

Analysis of people eliminating each other from suspicion by their presence in the lounge from time when Blane was known to be alive until he was reported missing.

At 7.45   Mrs. Jocelyn, Count Posodini, Mr. Rocksavage, Mr.
                 Stodart.

7.45 to 8.0   Steward, Rocksavage, Stodart.

8.0 to 8.5   Steward, Rocksavage, Stodart, the Bishop.

8.5 to 8.10   Steward, Rocksavage, Stodart, Bishop, Lady
                 Welter

8.10 to 8.15   Steward, Bishop, Stodart, Lady Welter.

8.15 to 8.25   Steward, Stodart, Bishop, Lady Welter, Mr. Hayashi.

8.25 to 8.30   Steward, Stodart, Bishop, Lady W., Hayashi, Posodini

8.30 to 8.32   Steward, Stodart, Bishop, Lady W., Hayashi, Posodini
                 and Mr. and Mrs. Jocelyn.

8.32 to 8.33   As above with cabin steward who reported Blane
                 missing.

UNVOUCHED FOR TIMES

The following table shows the number of minutes in the period 7.45 to 8.30, when each member of the party was not under direct observation of one of the others and, therefore, at liberty to commit the crime.

Mrs. Jocelyn.   In the lounge till 7.45.   Returned changed to lounge 8.30.   Unvouched for time full period of 45 minutes.

Count Posodini.   In lounge till 7.45.   Returned changed to lounge at 8.25.   Unvouched for time (in period) 40 minutes.

Mr. Rocksavage.   In lounge till 8.10.   Returned changed to lounge at 8.35.   Unvouched for time (in period) 20 minutes.

Mr. Stodart.   In lounge at 7.40.   Remained there till 8.33.   Unvouched for time (in period) nil.

Bishop of Bude.   Came below with Lady Welter at 7.5.   In lounge changed at 8.0.   Unvouched for time (in period) 15 minutes.

Lady Welter.   Came below with the Bishop at 7.5.   In lounge changed at 8.5.   Unvouched for time (in period) 20 minutes.

Mr Hayashi.   Went to cabin at 6.10.   In lounge changed at 8.15.   Unvouched for time (in period) 30 minutes.

Mr. Jocelyn.   Came below with Miss Rocksavage 7.30 (approx.) In lounge changed at 8.30.   Unvouched for time full period of 45 minutes.

Miss Rocksavage.   Came below with Mr. Jocelyn 7.15 (approx.) In lounge changed at 8.40.   Unvouched for time full period of 45 minutes.

DETECTIVE OFFICER KETTERING'S THIRD REPORT, CONTINUED.

The foregoing tables rule out the lounge steward, Cane, as he was only absent from the lounge for two periods of two minutes each during the time under review, and in each of these has to go down to Blane's cabin and come up again, and so he could not possibly have had time to perpetrate the crime in either.

The only other person who is entirely ruled out is the secretary, Nicholas Stodart, as he was in the lounge during the whole period under review.

Rocksavage and all his other guests were, however, absent from the lounge for periods of from 15 to 45 minutes between 7.45 and 8.30, during which they might have committed the murder.

I then proceeded to make an analysis of possible motives.

POSSIBLE MOTIVES

<u>Mrs. Jocelyn.</u>   Nil, as far as is known at the moment.

<u>Count Posodini.</u>   Nil, as far as is known at the moment.

<u>Mr. Rocksavage.</u>   Blane's death will send the shares of the Blane companies down to zero and, in their present precarious state, possibly cause them to crash altogether.   That would suit Rocksavage's book far better than the proposed amalgamation. Blane also stated his fear that Rocksavage might attempt his life, before he died.   Motive in Rocksavage's case is, therefore, strong.

<u>The Bishop of Bude.</u>   Nil, as far as is known at the moment.

<u>Lady Welter.</u>   As the largest holder in the Rocksavage

companies she stands to benefit by Blane's death.   She may have
other assets outside the Rocksavage companies, however, so,
although there is motive, in her case it is weak.

Mr. Hayashi.   Nil, as far as is known at the moment but,
as he is concerned in the world soap interest, he may well have
a motive which has not yet come to light.

Mr. Jocelyn.   Nil, as far as is known at the moment but,
as a dependent of Lady Welter, his interest marches with hers, so
it is possible that he might have acted at her instigation.

Miss Rocksavage.   Nil, as far as is known at the moment.

Having analysed the information gained from first
statements, as above, I then went below to examine the dead man's
property, an inventory of which follows:

**INVENTORY OF THE LATE BOLITHO BLANE'S PROPERTY FOUND IN
"C" SUITE OF S.Y. GOLDEN GULL.**

Contents of No. 1.   Louis Vuitton Wardrobe travelling trunk.

1.	Three piece dress suit.
1.	Three piece light grey tuxedo.
1.	Black dinner jacket.
1.	Cream shantung jacket.
3.	prs. White flannel trousers (clean).
3.	White dress waistcoats (clean).
5.	White dress shirts (clean).
6.	White dress ties (clean).
15.	White dress collars (clean).
11.	White turnover collars (clean).
1.	White silk dress muffler.
14.	White linen handkerchiefs (clean).
5.	Coloured silk shirts (clean).
4.	prs. Black dress socks (clean).
8.	prs. Coloured day socks (clean).
2.	Black dress bow ties.
15.	Coloured silk day ties.
7.	Silk Coloured handkerchiefs (clean).
1.	pr. Black silk suspenders.
2.	Suits silk underclothes, vests and pants (clean).
2.	prs. Silk pyjamas (clean).
1.	Panama hat.

Contents of No. 2.   Leather kit-bag.

4. Coloured short-sleeved sweat shirts (clean).
1. Pale yellow bath robe.
2. Two piece swimming suits.
1. Pr. rope soled beach shoes.
2. White dress shirts (dirty).
2. White dress ties (dirty).
1. White waistcoat (dirty).
2. White dress collars (dirty).
4. White turnover collars (dirty).
3. White linen handkerchiefs (dirty).
1. Suit, vest and pants silk underclothes (dirty).
2. Silk day shirts, coloured (dirty).
1. pr. Black dress silk socks (dirty).
2. prs. Coloured day socks (dirty).
2. Coloured silk handkerchiefs (dirty).
1. Bottle coconut oil (full).
1. Bottle Witch-hazel (full).

Contents of No. 3.   Louis Vuitton shoe trunk.

1. pr. Black patent dress shoes.
2. pr. Brown day shoes.
2. pr. White doeskin shoes.
2. Pots cleaning cream.
3. Cleaning brushes.
4. Leathers - cleaning.

Contents of No. 4.   Large leather fitted dressing case.

Papers various - all to do with Blane's companies.
1. Bottle bath salts.
1. Book - 'No Ordinary Virgin' by Eve Chaucer.
1. Nash's Magazine - current issue.
2. Tins (100 each) Balkan Sobranie cigarettes (unopened).
1. Bottle Gum Tragacanth.
7. Pencils - all sharpened.
2. India rubbers.
1. Bottle Phensic.
1. Bottle white powder (indigestion medicine).
1. Big silver flask containing brandy.
1. pr. Binoculars - Zeiss.
1. ·22 Scott Webley automatic (unloaded).
25. Bullets for same.
1. Electric torch.
68. Blank sheets foolscap.
1. Jewel box containing two sets diamond and black onyx
    waistcoat buttons, one set dress studs, one Lever
    (Sulka) collar fastener, various bone and metal studs,
    pins, waistcoat buckles and other oddments.

Blane's personal belongings already unpacked.

1. Dark blue belted overcoat.
1. Cording rainproof rubber coat.
1. Blue and green shot silk dressing gown.
1. pair soft leather slippers.
1. pair hairbrushes (from fitted case).
1. Comb (from fitted case).
1. Clothes brush (from fitted case).
1. Valet safety razor.
1. Shaving brush.
1. Bowl shaving soap.
1. Bottle hair oil (Douglas, Bond Street - half full).
1. Bath sponge.
1. Face flannel.
1. Tooth brush.
1. Plate brush.
1. Nail brush.
1. Black soft felt hat.
1. Box (opened) Balkan Sobranie cigarettes (38).
1. pr. Silk pyjamas (soiled).
1. Bottle Milton (three parts full).
1. Block yellow writing paper (25 sheets remaining).
1. Packet envelopes to match (10 only).
1. Bottle Parker fountain pen ink in travelling case.
2. Desk fountain pens in holders.
1. A card commencing "Dear Mr. Blane" found in right hand top dressing table drawer.

DETECTIVE OFFICER KETTERING'S THIRD REPORT, CONTINUED.

The last item on the inventory is of considerable interest as it comes from the Japanese, Inosuke Hayashi. It is on a yacht postcard and, therefore, written after Hayashi's arrival on board. Presumably it was delivered to Blane some time between his arrival on the yacht at 7.5 and his death, which is known to have occurred between 7.45 and 8.30. Postcard herewith.

S.Y. GOLDEN GULL.

Dear Mr. Blane.

Needless to say I was very shocked to receive your letter while I was in New York. You have certainly overlooked some considerations which are from your point of view extremely important, and quite apart from my own interests in the matter I consider it highly desirable that you should know the consequences to you of the action you contemplate before conferring with Mr. Rooksevage.

I shall be in my room until eight o'clock, but would prefer to discuss the matter in your room. Please, therefore, let me know at what time I may visit you.

Yours truly,

Isosuke Hayashi

DETECTIVE OFFICER KETTERING'S THIRD REPORT, CONTINUED.

With the assistance of Detective Officer Neame I then searched the cabins of all parties concerned. As the parties had slept in them on the previous night they had ample opportunity to destroy any incriminating evidence. However, as Blane's death was assumed to be suicide until early this morning, none of the innocent parties is likely to have taken any special precautions and, as in a case such as this, nearly everybody has some private peccadillo to conceal I was in hopes that we might still unearth some useful information which would eventually lead us to the murderer.

On my instructions to the Captain the whole party were informed, immediately each of them left their cabins this morning, that they were not to return to them until they received permission. None of the cabins had, therefore, been cleaned or tidied and each was locked after its occupant had gone up to breakfast.

The contents of the wastepaper baskets in each cabin, which had not been cleared since the previous morning, were removed and as a matter of routine their contents are being catalogued.

The search revealed items of interest in two cases only:-
Count Posodini - among the Count's belongings were found eight packs of specially prepared cards, two sets of loaded dice and an automatic Mouser .22 pistol with a silencer attached, one spare clip and 44 rounds of ammunition.

It will be recalled that, upon the Count's examination by me this morning, Detective Officer Neame remarked that he felt certain this man's face was familiar to him, and that we have him on our records.   The items above mentioned, having been discovered in his possession, give considerable colour to Detective Officer Neame's suggestion and every effort should be made to trace up particulars of this man at once.

The Bishop of Bude.   In a square black portable writing case belonging to the Bishop I found a letter which was evidently written and despatched by Bolitho Blane from New York and received by the Bishop in the post delivered to the yacht on her arrival off Miami yesterday.   Letter herewith.

HOTEL ADLON-CLARIDGE,
NEW YORK.

5th March 1936

My dear Bishop

I have only just learned that you are to make one of the party which Carleton Rockersavage is assembling on his yacht for a little holiday among the islands. It is, of course, many years since we met but I shall look forward so much to renewing my acquaintance with you.

You will, I am sure, recall those wonderfully interesting conversations which we held when we were together for a little time during the war. We established then a wonderful and, I feel, never to be forgotten friendship.

I have an idea that some very strange and unusual things are likely to take place upon Rockersavage's yacht once we put out to sea and, however strange these occurrences may be, I feel sure that you will bear in mind what very good friends we are. I value your friendship more than I can say and from your past expressions of esteem it makes me happy to think that you value mine equally highly

Yours very sincerely

Bolitho Blane

DETECTIVE OFFICER KETTERING'S THIRD REPORT, CONTINUED.

I then examined the ship's officers, Dr. Ackland, Mr. Rocksavage's personal physician, who messes with the officers, and all members of the crew.   I am satisfied none of them could have had any connection with the crime and take it you will not require detailed reasons for my conclusions.

As my examinations and listing of Blane's effects had occupied me all the morning, and a thorough search of the cabins of all parties some six hours, being completed a little after 8 o'clock, I decided to postpone any further examination of the parties until to-morrow morning, by which time it is to be hoped that further information about them from outside would be to hand.

Keys Kettering

Detective Officer
Florida Police.

8.25 p.m.   9.3.36.   on S.Y. Golden Gull.

Police Department.
Form GO/7431/N 58

POLICE HEADQUARTERS,
MIAMI,
FLA.

3.20 a.m. 10.3.36.

MEMO.

To Detective Officer Kettering.

I acknowledge herewith your two reports of yesterday's date, together with documents as stated therein. I am now forwarding herewith all information at present available regarding the parties concerned.

Let me have your report upon the re-examination of all parties, in the light of the fresh information obtained, as soon as possible.

John Nilton Schwab

Lieutenant
Florida Police.

IDENTIFICATION SECTION

Department of Police, New York City

Arrested July 4th 1930 in Mauretania on ship's arrival in New York.   Sentenced eighteen months for fraud.   Served fifteen months Sing Sing, then released for good conduct November 10th, 1931.

Arrested May 15th 1933, in Feldmar Hotel, N.Y.C. Sentenced two years for fraud.   Served twenty months Sing Sing, then released for good conduct January 28th, 1935.

Name   DANIELS GEORGE (SLICK).   Alias Phillip Vere-Frognal. Henri de Balasco. Count di Venuto. George Gordon-Carr.

Taken   28th February, 1935.

IDENTIFICATION SECTION

Department of Police, New York City

Name   DANIELS George (Slick)

Sex   **Male**   *Colour* **White**

Nationality   **U.S. citizen**   *Occupation* **Card sharp and con man**

Age **42**   *Height* **5ft.10½"**   *Weight* **149 lbs.**

Build **Medium**   *Complexion* **Dark**   *Hair* **Black - wavy**

Eyes **Brown**   *Eyebrows* **Bushy**   *Nose* **Straight**

Whiskers **Nil**   *Moustache* **Nil**   *Chin* **Pointed**

Face **Long oval**   *Neck* **Medium**   *Lips* **Thin upper**

Mouth **Straight**   *Head* **Well set**   *Ears* **Projecting**

Forehead **Square, double wrinkle**

Distinctive marks   **Deep lines from nostrils to mouth.**

Peculiarities   **Italian extraction. Good looking latin type. Often poses as foreign nobleman.**

Clothes   **Always smartly dressed but never flashy.**

Jewellery   **Gold signet ring on small finger, left hand**

Where likely to be found **Trades Atlantic ships**

Personal Associates   **Harry C. Rand. Mike Doolan. Phillipo Conetti Angela Forden.**

Habits   **Carries gun but never been known to use it. Smokes and drinks. Speaks Italian. Normally speaks English with American accent, but can almost hide any trace of accent when he wishes and sometimes passes as an Englishman.**

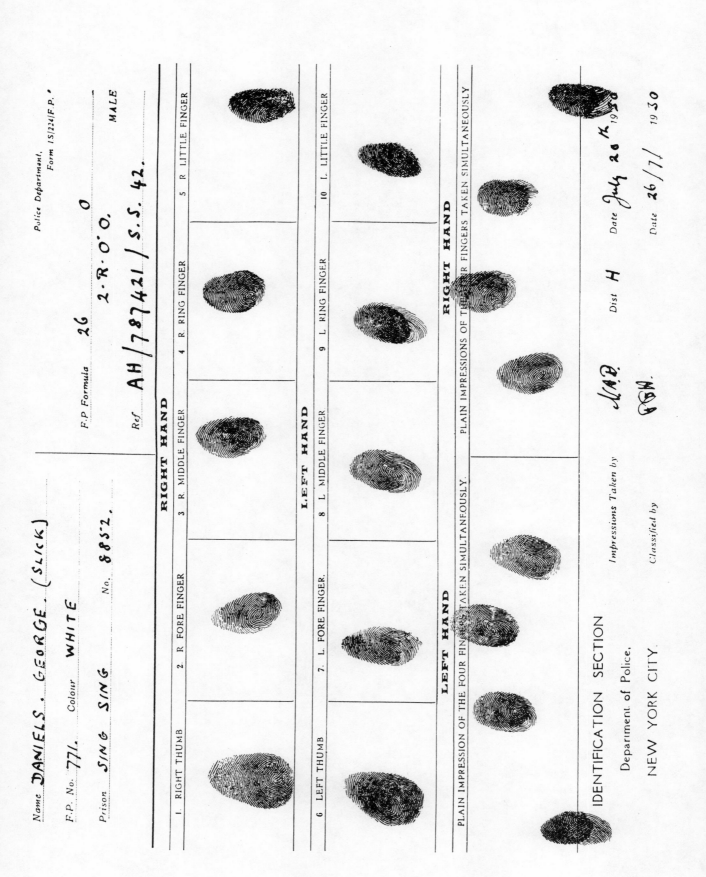

Police Department,
Form 1S/224/F.P.

Name DANIELS, GEORGE, (SLICK)

F.P. No. 771.   Colour WHITE

Prison SING SING   No. 885-2.

F.P. Formula   26   O
2·R·O·O.   MALE

Ref   AH/787421/S.S. 42.

RIGHT HAND

1. RIGHT THUMB	2. R. FORE FINGER	3. R. MIDDLE FINGER	4. R. RING FINGER	5. R. LITTLE FINGER

LEFT HAND

6. LEFT THUMB	7. L. FORE FINGER.	8. L. MIDDLE FINGER	9. L. RING FINGER	10. L. LITTLE FINGER

PLAIN IMPRESSION OF THE FOUR FINGERS TAKEN SIMULTANEOUSLY.

LEFT HAND

PLAIN IMPRESSIONS OF THE FOUR FINGERS TAKEN SIMULTANEOUSLY

RIGHT HAND

IDENTIFICATION SECTION
Department of Police,
NEW YORK CITY.

Impressions Taken by   M.A.B.   Dist H   Date July 26th 1930

Classified by   P.H.   Date 26/7/ 1930

FORM NO. 60.

WESTERN UNION
(THE WESTERN UNION TELEGRAPH COMPANY)
CABLEGRAM

ANGLO-AMERICAN TELEGRAPH Co., Ld.   CANADIAN NATIONAL TELEGRAPHS.

-9 MAR 36

M672 LONDON 408 10 0210 =

POLICE HEADQUARTERS MIAMIFLA =

YOUR ENQUIRY PQ 4726 LADY WELTER BORN AUGUST
EIGHTYONE WIDOW LATE SIR DAVID SHIPPING
MAGNATE DIED OCTOBER TWENTYTWO WILL ATTESTED
ONE MILLION THREE HUNDRED ELEVEN THOUSAND
STOP PURCHASED CONTROLLING INTEREST FIRESIDE
WEEKLY TWENTYTHREE CHRISTIAN GIRL TWENTYFIVE
CROSS AND PEN TWENTYEIGHT BRITISH YOUTH
TWENTYNINE ALL PAPERS HIGH MORAL TONE OBJECT
TO INFLUENCE BRITISH YOUTH TOWARDS ESTABLISHED
CHURCH LADY WELTER FANATIC ON THIS SUBJECT
STOP CIRCULATIONS OF PAPERS ONE EIGHT FIVE

NINETY ONE HUNDRED AND TWENTY AND TWO
HUNDRED AND FIFTY THOUSAND RESPECTIVELY ALL
RUN AT LOSSES MADE UP BY LADY WELTER
PRIVATELY STOP LADY WELTER INVOLVED HATREY
CRASH TWENTYNINE LOST LARGE PORTION OF
FORTUNE STOP PRINCIPAL INCOME NOW DERIVED
ROCKSAVAGE COMPANIES WHICH PASSED DIVIDENDS
LAST YEAR PAPERS NOW IN FINANCIAL DIFFICULTIES
STOP MANY FRIENDS IN HIGH POSITIONS
ESTABLISHED CHURCH INCLUDING BUDE STOP ONE
CHILD ONLY PAMELA MARY BORN SEPTEMBER
NINETEEN TEN EDUCATED ROEDEAN MARRIED NOVEMBER
THIRTYONE HON REGINALD JOCELYN NO CHILDREN
STOP HON MRS JOCELYN NO INFORMATION EXCEPT

ABOVE STOP HON REGINALD JOCELYN BORN MAY
NINETEEN TWO SECOND SON OF EARL OF CROCORN
EDUCATED ETON AND CAMBRIDGE ENTERED
STOCKBROKERS WRENN FALL AND HALKETT NINETEEN
TWENTYFIVE MOTOR SALESMAN RENDALL COMPANY
TWENTY SEVEN KENWENN ADVERTISING COMPANY
TWENTYEIGHT PUBLICITY DEPARTMENT PINNACLE FILMS
THIRTY MARRIED PAMELA WELTER THIRTYONE AND
ENTERED LADY WELTERS PUBLISHING HOUSE LATER
BECAME HER PERSONAL ADVISOR STOP NOT WELL
REGARDED BY FAMILY STOP NO PERSONAL FORTUNE
AS FAR AS ASCERTAINABLE STOP WRITTED FOR
DEBT MANY OCCASIONS BETWEEN TWENTYTHREE AND
THIRTYONE STOP APPARENTLY PROVIDED FOR SINCE

BY LADY WELTER STOP NICHOLAS STODART NO
INFORMATION STOP BISHOP OF BUDE BORN
SEVENTYONE EDUCATED PRIVATELY AND CARDIFF
UNIVERSITY ENTERED CHURCH NINETYTWO FROM
NINETYFIVE HAS CONTRIBUTED MANY ARTICLES
GENERAL PRESS ON CHURCH AFFAIRES STOP
NINETYNINE NINETEEN ONE SERVED AS PADRE SOUTH
AFRICAN WAR FOURTEEN SEVENTEEN WORLD WAR THEN
SENT HOME INVOLVED UNSAVOURY SCANDAL WITH
TROOPS ESCAPED PUBLICITY AS ENQUIRY HELD IN
PRIVATE AT WHICH BISHOP EXONORATED ON ALL
CHARGES APPOINTED SUFFRAGAN BISHOP SEPTEMBER
TWENTYTHREE STOP BISHOP OF BUDE MARCH
TWENTYNINE STOP BOLITHO BLANE DATE OF BIRTH

UNKNOWN AGE APPROXIMATELY FORTYEIGHT BELIEVED
TO HAVE ARRIVED EUROPE WITH AUSTRALIAN FORCES
DURING WORLD WAR STOP FIRST CAME INTO
PROMINENCE AS FINANCIER TWENTYTHREE STOP
TERMED BY PRESS MYSTERY MAN OF STOCK
EXCHANGE NO PHOTOGRAPHS EVER PUBLISHED STOP
LIVES AS RECLUSE BENWOOD COBHAM SURREY RARELY
VISITS LONDON OFFICES TRANSACTS BUSINESS BY
TELEPHONE STOP BLANE COMPANIES SHAKY AT
MOMENT SHREWD OBSERVERS BELIEVE HIM DUE CRASH
STOP COUNT POSODINI NO INFORMATION AVAILABLE
STOP =
CHIEF INSPECTOR TRING RECORDS SCOTLAND YARD ✲

INTELLIGENCE SECTION. (X.25.)

POLICE HEADQUARTERS,

MIAMI,

FLA.

9.3.36.

ONLY INFORMATION AVAILABLE AT THE MOMENT REGARDING MR. CARLTON
ROCKSAVAGE AND HIS DAUGHTER.

MR. ROCKSAVAGE.

From "WHO'S WHO IN THE U.S.A." 1936.

ROCKSAVAGE, Carlton Henry, b. Detroit, 17 Dec., 1876; 3rd s.
of late Theodore Henry and late Rose Emma; m. 1912,
Antoinette Gloria (d. 1928) o.c. of late Julius C. Pritchard
of Bridgeport, Con.; one d. Educ. Rudd College and
Technical Schools. Spears Cunliff Coy, 1898, Standard Oil
1904, Director Bloomberg & Frien, 1907, Managing Director,
1909. President Bloomberg Rocksavage, 1912. Chairman and
Managing Director Grandol Soaps, 1915. President Denton
Bros. in 1916. Formed Sen Toilet Preps., 1918. Founder and
President Rocksavage Inc., 1922. Rocksavage Con., 1933.
Recreations: yachting, golf. Address: 1482 Riverside Drive,
N.Y.C.: Lake House, Wading River, Long Island. T. RIV.
4827; WAD. 362. Clubs: Union, Grolier, New York Yacht,
Hython, Corinthian Yacht, Bevor Dam Sports; London,
American; Paris, Travellers.

Further to the above we have no police record, but the
following details are based on general information.
Carlton Rocksavage came of a respectable middle-class family
but, as a younger son, had to make his own way. On finishing his
education he entered the soap firm of Spears Cunliff and, six
years later, transferred to Standard Oil, in both of which he
gained considerable general experience. He left the latter to
become a director, again in soap, of Bloomberg Frien, a small
company of which he soon became the moving spirit. His rise to
eminence as a financier dates, however, from his marriage with
Antoinette Pritchard in 1912. Her father put up the necessary
capital and the firm was reorganised as Bloomberg Rocksavage in

INTELLIGENCE SECTION. (X.25.)

POLICE HEADQUARTERS,

MIAMI,

FLA.

the autumn of that year, with Rocksavage as president. The
company secured large contracts from the Allies for supplies in
the early stages of the war and it was in order to take advantage
of war contracts that Rocksavage assumed the chairmanship of
Grandol Soaps, which had their headquarters in Paris, in 1915.
The following year he also became president of Denton Bros. Inc.,
and by that time his financial interest was spreading in every
direction. Early in 1918 he formed Sen Toilet Preparations to
handle other lines allied to the soap industry and at the
conclusion of the war he was reputed to be worth a very considerable
fortune. His companies suffered somewhat in the after-war slump
but various retrenchments were effected and his business continued
to develop in all parts of the world, until the depression set
in. 1932, however, found him in very serious difficulties and it
was rumoured then that he might go under. His original partner,
Mostyn Bloomberg, died in the November of that year. The cause
of his death was never cleared up quite satisfactorily. He was
found dead in his office chair one afternoon and poison of a
subtle variety, which would leave little trace, was suspected. It
is believed, however, that, if this was the case, the poison was
self-administered as Bloomberg, in addition to having a large and
expensive family, had lived with the utmost extravagance for many
years, and had come to the end of his financial resources. No
suspicion attaches to Rocksavage in this matter, although he was
present in the same block of offices at the time. After his
partner's death he reorganised as Rocksavage Consolidated in
January, 1933, and then succeeded in bringing his companies
through the depression. He has, however, never regained his
financial strength and last year has shown a steady decline in the
shares of those concerns in which he is interested. This is
largely due to a price cutting war which he has been waging with
the British soap group, controlled by Bolitho Blane.

INTELLIGENCE SECTION. (X.25.)

POLICE HEADQUARTERS,

MIAMI,

FLA.

MISS FERRI ROCKSAVAGE.

Only child of the above.   Born 10.5.1913.   Educated Heath
Hurst School, Long Island, Munich and Paris.   Prominent socialite
and member of the young New York Smart Set.   On her return from
Europe four years ago she at once became a press personality.   Is
fond of amateur acting and has appeared at nearly all smart
charity shows in recent years.   Much photographed and credited
with numerous love affairs.   There are grounds to suppose that
the Wendel-Norton marriage was broken up on her account, although
she was not cited as co-respondent.   Last fall she was constantly
in company with well-known film star, Jack Houghton, and there
were rumours of her engagement to him at the time, but nothing
came of this.   She often accompanies her father upon his yachting
trips and does hostess at the big private entertainments which he
gives in his New York and Long Island homes.   She is often absent
at house parties, however, and lives the independent life of a
modern young woman.

WESTERN UNION

(THE WESTERN UNION TELEGRAPH COMPANY)

CABLEGRAM

ANGLO-AMERICAN TELEGRAPH Co., Ld   CANADIAN NATIONAL TELEGRAPHS.

-9 MAR 36

TOKIO 46 10 1130 -

POLICE HEADQUARTERS MIAMIFLA =

INOSUKE HAYASHI NATIVE OF NAGASAKI EDUCATED

OXFORD AGE THIRTYFIVE STOP HAS NEGOTIATED

MANY COMMERCIAL TRANSACTIONS FOR JAPANESE

GOVERNMENT STOP BELIEVED ACTING AT MOMENT

SHIKOKU PRODUCTS COMPANY WHO HAVE BIG

DEALINGS WITH OFFICE OF INTERIOR SUPPLIES

DEPARTMENT STOP =

TAKASHI INFORMATION BUREAU

POLICE HEADQUARTERS TOKYO ⚓

DETECTIVE OFFICER KETTERING'S FOURTH REPORT.

I have to acknowledge your memo. of to-day's date, together with cabled report from Scotland Yard upon Mr. Blane, the Bishop of Bude, Lady Welter and Mr. and Mrs. Jocelyn ; also about Mr. Hayashi from the Japanese police; the identification particulars of George ("Slick") Daniels, alias Count Posodini; and the information supplied by you about Mr. and Miss Rocksavage.

Last night I decided that it would be a good thing to have a talk with Nicholas Stodart in order to find out from him as many particulars as possible about Blane's life and affairs.   I therefore suggested that he should join me for dinner as all my meals are served separately in the small writing room in which I am conducting my examinations.

He agreed readily enough, but the meal did not prove a particularly happy one as Stodart has a small abscess and, on account of this, is suffering somewhat with his false teeth, which give him pain when eating solids.   He is also very distressed by his employer's death which leaves him without a situation, and I gather, very little money.   He talked quite freely, however, and the following is such information as I gleaned from this interview.

PARTICULARS GATHERED FROM A TALK WITH BLANE'S SECRETARY, NICHOLAS STODART.

Blane was a generous, but difficult, employer.   The work which he demanded of his secretary was light but, on the other hand, he liked to have him at his beck and call the whole time, and part of the understanding on Stodart's engagement was that, except in very special circumstances, he would not be allowed any free time off duty

This suited Stodart as he is quite alone in the world and has no relatives or friends whom he wished to visit.

His history is as follows:- He is 46 years of age and was born at Felixstowe, Suffolk, England. His mother died at the time of his birth and his father was employed in the Indian Forestry Department. During his early childhood Stodart lived with a maiden aunt, the sole surviving member of his mother's family, to whom she had come home when she was about to have her baby. The aunt was killed in a railway accident, however, when Stodart was eight years of age, and so he was sent to a boarding school in Felixstowe and he never saw his father, except during four periods of leave at intervals of several years, until he was sixteen, when he left school and went out to live with his father in India.

For the next few years he studied accountancy and, having served an apprenticeship with Messrs. Wayne, Robins & Co., of Calcutta, he succeeded in obtaining a position with the Ranaga Rubber Company. His duties with this company entailed visits to numerous rubber plantations owned by the company, where he spent anything from a week to a fortnight inspecting the accounts on the spot twice yearly, and then moved on to another station. His friends, therefore, consisted solely of planters that he visited twice yearly, since he was never able to settle down for any lengthy period in one place and create a permanent circle of friends.

He enlisted in 1914, but was not sent home, being drafted as one of the reserves to the India Frontier Force, and thus spent the whole of his war service in northern India.   His father died in 1917 and Stodart was disappointed to find that his father left practically nothing.   He had always assumed that, as his father could spend very little in his isolated forest station he must be saving a good portion of his salary, but on Stodart senior's death, it was found that he was an inveterate gambler and had invested all his savings in various companies which held out prospects of enormous dividends from oil, gold, etc., but proved to be worthless concerns.   His father's death did not improve Stodart's position, therefore, and he was not able to save very much out of his moderate salary.

He received promotion in his firm from time to time but never rose higher in it than deputy accountant at a salary of £600 a year.   Then he suffered a big set back because his firm went under in 1931, owing to world depression, so he found himself out of a job at the age of 41.

He remained in India for a further two years, partly living on his savings and partly by temporary work which he managed to obtain with one or two firms in rush periods.

Early in 1934 he decided that the prospects of earning his living in India were becoming more and more hazardous and so he decided to return to his mother country. There, however, he did not meet with any better fortune as there were few openings for men of his age and scope. Until early this year he managed to support himself by taking various temporary clerical posts, but he had practically exhausted his savings, and was in a pretty bad way, when he noticed an advertisement in a local paper.

The advertiser offered a permanent post with good remuneration to a man free of all responsibilities, who was prepared to travel if necessary. Qualifications demanded were that the applicant should be under fifty, but have had at least twenty years' experience in a secretarial post, or as an executive in a business office. Public school education not essential but must possess decent manners and appearance.

The advertisement appeared in the East Anglian Times and applicants were asked to apply to a Mr. Benwood at the White Horse Hotel, Ipswich. Stodart was staying in the town at the time, so he called and managed to secure the job.

Having taken him on, Benwood explained that his real name was Bolitho Blane but he had not advertised under his real name in order to avoid unnecessary publicity. He took Stodart off the next day to his home at Cobham in Surrey. For the next fortnight Stodart acted as Blane's Secretary but his duties were very light as Blane did nearly all his business over the wire, and never went to London. Stodart, in fact, was never even called on to visit the London offices of Blane's companies, nor did he meet any of Blane's executives as, during this period, none of them came down to see him.

In the latter part of February Blane informed Stodart that they would shortly be leaving for the United States and explained the reason for his decision to make the trip. By that time Stodart, of course, had acquired a certain knowledge of Blane's situation and his financial position, so he was competent to undertake the secretarial work which Blane gave him on the voyage over.

Stodart says himself that it seemed queer Blane should take on a complete stranger for this job of secretary with very little knowledge about him, but he thinks that Blane already had the American trip in mind when he engaged him and was anxious to have somebody with him who was capable of doing the odd jobs in connection with his journey and, at the same time, competent to take accurate notes of his conference with Rocksavage, yet someone completely outside his business, so that there could not possibly be any leakage of information about what occurred at the conference to any of his other employees in his London office.

DETECTIVE OFFICER KETTERING'S FOURTH REPORT, CONTINUED.

This morning, immediately I received the outside information upon various members of the party I proceeded to a new analysis of the situation and composed a fresh draft of possible motives.

POSSIBLE MOTIVES. 10.3.36.

Mrs. Jocelyn. Nil, as far as is known at the moment.

Count Posodini. Nil, as far as is known at the moment, but the Count is now identified as the ex-convict "Slick" Daniels, so

I hope to be able to make him talk, as there must be some special reason for Reginald Jocelyn having asked him on board, when he was quite unknown to any other member of the party.

Mr. Rocksavage. Strong motive to do away with Blane, as pointed out in previous analysis. This becoming even stronger on confirmation of the precarious situation of his companies.

The Bishop of Bude. Nil, as far as is known at the moment, but his possession of a letter from Blane mailed from New York on the 5th shows his acquaintance with the murdered man to be far stronger than he would have us believe in his first statement. This letter lays such stress upon the friendship existing between the two that it reads to me much more like a threat by Blane that, whatever might occur in the yacht, the Bishop had better keep his mouth shut.   This is supported by the suggestion in the cable from Scotland Yard that there was some unpleasant scandal in which the Bishop was involved in 1917.

Lady Welter. Motive in her case, which was weak in our first analysis, is considerably strengthened by the cable from Scotland Yard, in which it appears that she has been expending a portion of her fortune for numerous years in supporting a non-commercial group of papers.   Further, that she lost a considerable portion of her capital in the Hatry crash, and is now principally dependent upon her holdings in the Rocksavage companies.

Mr. Hayashi. Nil, as far as is known at the moment, but the fact that he wrote to Blane, asking for an appointment, brings him

much more strongly under suspicion.   If it can be proved that he
visited Blane's cabin between 7.45 and 8.15, when he appeared in
the lounge, it will look very much as though he is our man.

Mr. Jocelyn. As dependent of Lady Welter his motive is
considerably strengthened by the facts about her financial
situation which have now emerged.   From the report of his
activities previous to his marriage with Lady Welter's daughter
it is obvious that he is something of an adventurer and, since
he was frequently writted, probably unscrupulous where money is
concerned.   Moreover, he is responsible for having introduced in
to the party a known criminal, "Slick" Daniels, alias Count
Posodini.

Miss Rocksavage. Nil, as far as is known at the moment.
I then proceeded to re-examine the whole party.

DETECTIVE OFFICER NEAME'S SHORTHAND NOTES OF DETECTIVE OFFICER KETTERING'S SECOND EXAMINATION OF COUNT POSODINI.

K.   Good morning, Count.

P.   Hallo, hallo, still busy Mr. Sherlock Holmes?

K.   Very busy indeed, Mr. Daniels.

P.   Well, now, just fancy your people being as quick off the mark as all that.

K.   You don't deny it?

P.   What's the use, friend? I kept up the little bluff yesterday because I had half a hope that you might lay your hands on the man who gave Blane his rightaway. Then I could have gone back to business without any sort of trouble from you folk at all but it was only half a hope and I knew that if you didn't get your man you'd pick it up that the Count stuff was all hooey by to-day.

K.   Well, that's frank, anyhow. Now, what do you know ?

P.   I don't know nothing. I swear by Almighty God ....

K.   Cut it Slick, cut it. You're in a spot. You know that, don't you?

P.   So that's the line, is it - trying to frame me, are you?

K.   Not a bit of it. I want your help, that's all.

P.   Oh, yeah! That's what all you guys say, and once I start to shoot my mouth I'll say something I didn't mean, then you'll be on me and I'll be for the hotsquat before I know what's happened. No sir. I'm not talking.

K.   Now, look here, Slick, I'm not trying to frame you - honest. But you're in a jam, boy - in a jam. You're an old timer, mixing

in with this swell crowd.   Why?   You didn't come here for sunbathing and big-game fishing, and you didn't come here to invest
a million dollars in soap.   What's more, you've got a gun down in
your cabin.

P.   There you are - what did I say?   Just because I'm known to
the bulls you're jumping to it that I bumped off Blane.   What's
a gun, anyway?   Your bunch have never known me use one, have
they?

K.   No, that's the whole point.   Murder is not your racket,
Slick, so you've got nothing to be frightened of if you'll come
clean, but if you don't, Slick, you're in a spot; you're in a spot
my boy.

P.   You've said a mouthful.   If you can't get the right guy
you'll get the wrong, rather than fall down on your job, and
having me on board makes it easy money.

K.   You know how things pan out, Slick.   It's a bad break, but
that's just how it might be.

P.   Will you play ball with me, if I play ball with you?

K.   Sure I will, Slick.   I know you didn't do it.   You're a
con man and a sharp.   This isn't your racket, but you've got to
tell me just what you know.

P.   O.K.   Shoot the questions.

K.   You were in the lounge until 7.45 the night before last with
Mrs. Jocelyn, then, according to your previous statement, you both
went below together.   You turned up in the lounge again at 25
after 8.   It doesn't take a man forty minutes to change his

clothes and I want to know just what you did during that time.

P.   Well, it was this way, chief: that dame's sweet on me.

K.   Which dame?

P.   Why, Mrs. Jocelyn.   She's a good looker, too, but I make it a rule never to mix business with pleasure.

K.   So you were here on business?

P.   There you are, what did I say?   You'll have me on the hot squat before I know which way I'm walking.   You bulls are all the same.

K.   Oh, forget it.   Go on now.   You say this dame is sweet on you?

P.   Yes, she made just one darn nuisance of herself ever since the day after we put out from New York.   "Oh, Count, it's such a lovely day, would you carry my rug up to the sun deck ?" - "Oh, Count, don't run away, there 're so many things I want to talk to you about." - "Oh, Count, must you go below, then let's meet in the lounge before the others come up for a cocktail."   Well, it's all right when you want that sort of thing, but when you don't some janes give you the willies.

K.   I get you.   Now let's go back to the night in question.

P.   Well, it was this way: when we were talking in the lounge, before Rocksavage and that fellow Stodart came in, I happened to have mentioned that I had read a real good book, "The Saint in New York," it was called, by a guy named Charteris.   When we came down the companion-way she said to me, 'Oh, Count, I wonder if you'd lend me that lovely book you've **just finished** ?" and she takes my arm and accompanies me along to my cabin. I handed her the book immediately we got inside but she wasn't going. Oh, no, sir, believe you me. She wanted something much more exciting than the "Saint in New York." Down she sat on the edge of my bed and engaged me in conversation.

K. Only conversation?

P. Sure! Haven't I been telling you. She sat there nearly half an hour, and even then I had my work cut out to get rid of her. Then I had to scram after she left, or I wouldn't have been changed in time for dinner. That's all there is to it.

K. Right, that's fine. Now, I want to know why Reginald Jocelyn asked you to join this party in the first place?

P. He fancies himself at poker, so he asked me along in the hope we'd be able to make a little school and brighten up the trip.

K. Was he in it that you were a sharp?

P. Well, no, I wouldn't say that, but he's no fool, that boy, although I certainly took a wad off him when we crossed together in the Normandie. He can see as far as most people and, although he's no reason to complain, I wouldn't be surprised if he thinks my castle in Italy to be all moonshine.

K. Listen, Slick: he wouldn't have asked you to come along if he felt that way about you, and it's pretty obvious from what you say that he did. There must have been some other reason and I want it.

P. Well, if there was, I'm not talking about it.

K.   Don't you think it would be better to do the talking quietly here with me, than to some heartless cop you'll have to spill the beans to if I send you ashore?

P.   You wouldn't do that, chief.

K.   I would, and you know it.   You're due for a first class grilling, Slick, unless you come clean with me.

P.   If only you'll believe me, that's all I ask.

K.   I'll believe you all right.   Now let's have it.

P.   Well, Jocelyn and I got friendly in the Normandie, and one night I asked him if he ever did a job of work, or just drifted around being the grand play boy all the time.   He told me he was in Lady Welter's outfit, and from then on we got to talking stocks and shares.   He let it out that most of his ma-in-law's money was tied up in the Rocksavage companies and they hadn't been doing too well lately, because Bolitho Blane and his crowd had been hitting into them right and left.

At the mention of Bolitho Blane I just saw red.   I've never seen the man.   Honest, chief, I never have, but he did me dirt once that I'll never forget.   He came on board the old Mauretania to see somebody off at Liverpool, and he noticed me among the passengers.   He recognised me from a snapshot that had been taken on a previous trip when I got intimate with a friend of his and - well - you know my line of business Chief, I had skinned that friend of his good and grand.   He tipped off the purser.   The purser told me, afterwards, that he had.   They watched me specially during that trip and caught me out.   That was the first time and the judge sent me down for eighteen months in Sing Sing.

Now, I ask you, wasn't that just a devilish trick to play. It wasn't as though I had taken a wad off Blane himself, but he must go and point me out to the purser as a suspect, and that put me behind the bars.   I've always sworn that I'd get even with him one day.

K.   So that's how the land lies, is it?

P.   No, no, Chief, you've got me all wrong.   Didn't I say that once a guy starts talking he lets himself in.   I didn't murder Blane.   I give you my word I didn't.

K.   I'm not suggesting that you did, but now you've got so far you'd better give me the rest of the story.

P.   All right, then.   When I went off the deep end about Blane this chap Jocelyn became mighty interested and he said to me, "Now, if you'd really like a chance to settle your account with Blane I can give it you.   A little party is being arranged in about a fortnight's time in Mr. Rocksavage's yacht, for deep-sea fishing, sunbathing and that sort of thing.   Blane is going to be one of the guests.   Would you care to come along?"

Well, I thought that over.   I didn't give Blane his, I swear I didn't.   That was the last thing in my mind.   But it seemed a grand opportunity to get in with the swell crowd, like this.

K.   How's the luck been running?

P.   I haven't touched a card since I came on board.   There's been a little mild bridge evenings, that's all.   What d'you take me for anyway?   Think I'd go and spill the beans by soaking this crowd for a few grand first evening we were out of port.   No, sir!   That's not the kind of man I am.   There might have been just one little card party one night before we got back to port, where maybe I'd have been the lucky one, but not so lucky that any of these people would ever have supposed there was anything phoney about me.   I valued this connection higher than that.   If I played my hand right on this trip it was a sure bet they'd be asking me parties when we got back to New York.   That's what I was after, and I wasn't going to spoil it by any funny stuff on the trip.

K.   Has Jocelyn said anything to you since you came on board about the chance he had given you to settle accounts with Blane?

P.   Not a thing.   I just took him at his word and came along and, if you want the truth, by the time we were one day out I'd just forgotten every word about that conversation in the Normandie.   I was so interested in making these new hook ups with the society crowd that I'd even forgotten Blane was coming on board until his secretary introduced himself to Rocksavage two evenings ago just after we sailed from Miami.

K.   You do believe though that Jocelyn asked you on board principally because he knew that you had a grudge against Blane?

P.   That's God's truth, Chief - God's truth, and if you ask me something fresh must have happened to make Jocelyn so mad with Blane that he sailed in and did the job himself before waiting to see if I'd act as his catspaw.

K.   All right, Slick, that'll do now.   I'll be seeing you.

Police Department.

Form RL/2120/C.7.

<u>DETECTIVE OFFICER NEAME'S SHORTHAND NOTES OF DETECTIVE OFFICER</u>

<u>KETTERING'S SECOND EXAMINATION OF THE HONOURABLE MRS. REGINALD</u>

<u>JOCELYN.</u>

K.   Good morning, Mrs. Jocelyn.

P.J.   Good morning.

K.   Sit down won't you.   There are just a few more things I want to ask you about the night before last.

P.J.   Thanks - but I have already told you all I know.

K.   All, Mrs. Jocelyn?   I wish I could be quite certain about that.

P.J.   But aren't you?   Whyever not?   I don't know anything about Mr. Blane's death at all.

K.   Maybe you don't, but I just want you to think very carefully.   Forget anything which you may have said to me yesterday.   Put it right out of your head and I promise I won't hold it against you.   I want you to tell me exactly where you were in this yacht between the time of your leaving the lounge with Count Posodini and returning to it changed for dinner on the night before last.

P.J.   But I've already told you.   I came below with the Count, left him at his cabin door and went straight along to my own cabin to change.   My husband can prove that because he was there - lying in his bath - when I came in.

K.   Ever read a book called 'The Saint in New York,' by Leslie Charteris, Mrs. Jocelyn?

P.J.   Oh, er - yes I am reading it at the moment, but I suppose you saw it in my cabin when you searched the whole ship yesterday.

K.   That's right, where did you get that book?

P.J.   Count Posodini lent it to me.

K   When?

P.J.   Well, as a matter of fact, it was the evening that we're talking about.   He gave it to me just after we came below, and I took it to my cabin when I went to change.

K.   That's better.   Now we're getting somewhere.   How long did you stay in the Count's cabin?

P.J.   I was never in it.   He went in and got the book and handed it out to me through the door.

K.   Now, Mrs. Jocelyn, this won't do.   I have no desire to pry into your private life, and if you've been having an affair with the Count that's nobody's business.   Anything you say is just confidential between you and me, but you've got to tell me the truth because somebody on this ship has committed murder, and somebody is going to the electric chair on that account.   You'd feel pretty bad if that somebody was the wrong person; just because you failed to own up to it that you were talking to them while the murder was being committed, and you were the only alibi they had - wouldn't you?

P.J.   Please don't let's be melodramatic, Inspector.   I'm sure it won't come to that and, as I've already told you, my husband can prove I was in my cabin at 7.45.   He asked me the time as I came into the bathroom and I looked at my watch.

K.   I am sorry but I don't believe you, Mrs. Jocelyn.   It's natural enough that you and your husband should have got together directly it was discovered that there had been a murder done on board.   You fixed that time between you to coincide with the time you left the lounge but, at the time you say you found your husband in the bath, you weren't in your own suite at all.

P.J.   Well, if you choose to think I'm a liar .... but I don't admit that I am for one moment.

K.   I see.   That's your story and you're sticking to it.   All right, Mrs. Jocelyn.   I won't trouble you any more for the moment, but later on I'm afraid you may be sorry that you haven't seen your way to tell me the truth.

P.J.   It is the truth, I tell you.

K.   So you say, sister, but I don't believe you, so there's no use our arguing any more about it.   You can go now .... no, not that way.   D'you mind going into the next cabin and waiting there for a few moments.   I'm going to have a little talk with your husband next, and I'd prefer that you shouldn't have any opportunity of comparing notes with him as you pass each other in the passage-way .... Thanks.

DETECTIVE OFFICER NEAME'S SHORTHAND NOTES OF DETECTIVE OFFICER

KETTERING'S THIRD EXAMINATION OF THE HONOURABLE REGINALD JOCELYN.

K.   Good morning, Mr. Jocelyn.

J.   Good morning, Officer.

K.   There are just a few more things I want to ask you about the series of events which preceded the discovery of Bolitho Blane's death.

J.   Right'o, fire away.

K.   According to your previous statements, you were on deck with Miss Rocksavage when the yacht sailed from Miami.   You both went below together, but in your statements the times vary.   You say that you came down to your cabin at 7.30, whereas Miss Rocksavage says that you both came down at 7.15.   Can you get any nearer to the actual time for me ?

J.   I don't think so.   You know what life is in pleasant company on board a ship.   When you're enjoying yourself time goes only too quickly.   It's always time to have a swim, or go in to lunch, or change for dinner, or something.

K.   I see.   You find Miss Rocksavage's company very enjoyable then?

J.   Certainly.   She's a very amusing and intelligent young woman, and, incidentally, she's my hostess, and so it is her due that I should devote a certain amount of my time to her.   In this particular case the duty happens to be a very pleasant one. That's all.

K.   I see.   You can't get nearer to the time you went below

than that it might have been 7.15 or it might have been 7.30,
then?

J.   No.   If Miss Rocksavage said it was 7.15 I don't doubt
she's right.

K.   Very well, let's agree that was so.   You went below at 7.15
and you did not arrive changed in the lounge until 8.30.   That is
an hour and a quarter.   You don't mean to tell me that it took
you all that time to change.

J.   Dear, dear, dear.   How pernicketty you policemen are.   We
went into all this yesterday morning and I told you then that I
always take my time about changing.   Moreover, that I often spend
a long time lying in my bath.

K.   Can you tell me how long you spent in your bath on the
evening in question?

J.   Not exactly, but I was already in it at a quarter to eight
because my wife came down from the lounge at that time and I asked
her what time it was as she came into the cabin.

K.   And she told you 7.45?   I find that very interesting.

J.   Why?

K.   You'll find out friend before this enquiry is over.   Now,
it was at your invitation that Count Posodini joined this party,
wasn't it?

J.   Yes.

K.   D'you mind telling me when it was that you tumbled to it
that the Count was a crook?

J.   What the hell d'you mean?

K.   Just what I say.   Count Posodini is known to the police and his intimates as "Slick" Daniels, card sharp and con man, who trades the Atlantic ships.   Would you like me to tell you just the sum that "Slick" took off you in the Normandie before you tumbled to it that he was a crook?

J.   I see.   Posodini is a crook and you found him out, then jumped to it that he murdered Blane so, to protect himself, he's faked up some cock and bull story involving me, has he?   Well, officer, that won't wash, and you needn't think it will.   I had not the least reason in the world to wish any ill to Blane and very fortunately for me, as it happens, my wife can prove that I was lying in my bath at 7.45, when we all know that Blane was still alive from the fact that he scribbled something on the back of the note that was sent down to him at that time.

K.   How d'you know that?

J.   Mr. Rocksavage told me and, if you don't mind not inter-rupting, as I was about to add, my wife having been with me in our suite from 7.45 until we arrived in the lounge at 8.30 together, that proves quite conclusively that I had no hand in Blane's death.

K.   Does it, Mr. Jocelyn? I wonder. I am quite satisfied that "Slick" didn't do this job. Murder is absolutely outside his line of country, whatever he may have led you to suppose when you had your little talk about Blane in the Normandie.

J.   I suppose that's another portion of Posodini's cock and bull story.

K.   Mr. Jocelyn, it happens to have been my job to spend a good
portion of my life examining the criminal classes and so officers
like myself get a sort of feeling as to when they're telling the
truth and when they're not.   It's my belief that "Slick" has
come clean with me and, in any case, I'm pretty satisfied about
his movements during the time under review, so I think you'd
better count him out.   Now, if we accept his story, it seems that
you invited him on board, knowing him to be no better than he
should be, and knowing too that he had a definite grudge against
Bolitho Blane.   He took advantage of your invitation because it
gave him the opportunity to mix with a swell crowd where he might
have picked up a lot of loose money, but if we're to believe his
statement you had far more cause to wish Blane out of the way than
he had.   You're in a pretty bad spot, Mr. Jocelyn, and I think the
time has come when you'd better stop lying and tell the truth.

J.   You - you're not really suggesting that I murdered Blane,
are you?

K.   I am.

J.   But - but, this is fantastic.   Besides I've already told
you that my wife can prove that she found me in my bath at 7.45,
and that we were never out of each other's sight from that time
on, until we went up to dinner at 8.30.

K.   I have just advised you to stop lying, Mr. Jocelyn.   Your
wife did not find you in your bath at 7.45, because she was
somewhere else at that time, and for the best part of half an hour
onwards.   During that time I don't know where you were, but it

may quite well have been in Blane's cabin.   In fact it's going to look like that unless you can provide some other explanation as to how you were spending your time.

J.   I was in my bath, I tell you.   All I know is that when my wife came into the cabin, I asked her the time and she said that it was 7.45.   She may have been wrong.   It may have been much later. How the hell do I know.

K.   If it was much later, that doesn't improve your situation, because you definitely wanted Blane out of the way and, unless you can bring evidence to show what you were doing between 7.45 and 8.15, I must assume that, since you've lied to me on other matters, you're lying now, and that you were in Blane's cabin.

J.   Now look here, Officer, whether my wife was right or wrong about the time I don't know, but one thing that stands out a mile is that there is a man on board this yacht who had far more reason to wish Blane out of the way than ever I had.

K.   Who?

J.   Why, Rocksavage, of course.   Two days ago he was bankrupt. Now that Blane's shares have gone to pot, as anybody knew they would the moment he was dead, Rocksavage has been buying every share in the Blane companies as they come on the market.   He was picking up Argus Suds at $17\frac{1}{4}$ yesterday, and Redmeyer Syndicates at 32.   He's standing in to make a fortune over this thing, because once Blane's death had been announced he was able to get all the financial backing he needed without the least trouble, whereas nobody would loan him a bob for the last fifteen months.   He has

the whole of the world soap interest in his pocket to-day.   Don't
you realise that?   And the thing he's got to thank for it is
Blane's death.

K.   Yes, I see that, but there's one point you seem to have
forgotten, or perhaps you didn't know it, because you wouldn't
have the same opportunity as I've had to check up on these time
sheets.   Rocksavage did not leave the lounge to go below and
change until 8.10 and even then he wasn't back in the lounge until
8.35, five minutes late for dinner.   A man could hardly have
changed in that time if he had murdered another man and had to
dispose of the body and wash a blood stain out of the carpet, too.

J.   Couldn't he?   That's all you know.   Rocksavage could.
Believe you me.

K.   Why?

J.   Only the night before we reached Miami he was prepared to
bet anybody that he could change for dinner in under four minutes.
The Count, or "Slick" as you call him, took him on.   A hundred
dollars even money and Rocksavage won the bet.   He was back in
the lounge changed again under four minutes after he left us.   If
he could do it then, he could do it again the following night,
when somebody put "paid" to Blane's account.   If Rocksavage
changed in four minutes that night he would still have had twenty
minutes free to do Blane in.

K.   Thank you, Mr. Jocelyn.   I find that very interesting.
That will be all for the moment.

DETECTIVE OFFICER NEAME'S SHORTHAND NOTES OF DETECTIVE OFFICER

KETTERING'S SECOND EXAMINATION OF MISS FERRI ROCKSAVAGE.

K.   Good morning, Miss Rocksavage.

F.R.   Good morning.

K.   Sorry to trouble you again but there's just a little
difference of opinion between Mr. Jocelyn and yourself as to what
time you came down from the top deck on the evening of Blane's
death.   He says it was 7.30 and you say it was 7.15.   Can you
clear that up for me?

F.R.   I'm afraid not.   I didn't really notice the time and perhaps
it was twenty or twenty-five past seven, but surely you're not
suggesting that I had anything to ......

K.   Of course not, Miss Rocksavage, of course not.   But saying
it was even as late as 7.25 you didn't get into the lounge
changed until 8.40.   That is an hour and a quarter after you came
below.   Surely that's a long time for even a lady to take
changing for dinner.

F.R.   But I told you yesterday that I didn't start to change at
once.   I was reading a book in my cabin for half an hour or so
after I came down.

K.   Yes, I remember that, but as you had so much spare time on
your hands it seems a little strange that you should have been ten
minutes late for dinner.

F.R.   I was interested in my book and I forgot the time.   You
must know how easy it is to do that if you are deep in an exciting
story.   My maid will tell you that I did not ring for her until

nearly a quarter past eight.   That's why I was late.

K.   I see, and you did not see Mr. Jocelyn again after, say,
7.30 at the latest, until you reached the lounge at 8.40?

F.R.   Why do you ask that?

K.   Well, I'm just going to let you in on something, Miss
Rocksavage, which I want you to keep to yourself.   It's not your
movements that I'm interested in but Mr. Jocelyn's.

F.R.   You don't think . . . .

K.   I don't know, Miss Rocksavage, but unless he can bring
somebody forward to vouch for what he was up to between 7.30 and
8.10 things aren't going to look too good for him.   If, on the
other hand, you were with him for longer than you say we'd forget
your previous statement, and that might make just all the
difference as far as he's concerned.

F.R.   No, no.   I wasn't with him after, say, 7.30 at the latest.

K.   All right, Miss Rocksavage, thank you.

Police Department.
Form RL/2120/C.7.

DETECTIVE OFFICER NEAME'S SHORTHAND NOTES OF DETECTIVE OFFICER
KETTERING'S EXAMINATION OF MISS ROCKSAVAGE'S MAID, NELLIE ORDE.

K.   Come in.   Don't look so scared now.   I'm not going to
bite you.   Sit down kid.

O.   Oh, I'm not scared.

K.   That's the way.   Now, you're Miss Rocksavage's maid,
aren't you ?   D'you help her to dress every evening?

O.   Yes.

K.   Did you help her the night that Blane got his?

O.   Yes.

K.   How long were you with her?

O.   She rang for me about ten after eight and we weren't through
till near a quarter of nine.

K.   How d'you find her when you came along?

O.   All right.   She's always cheerful.   I'll give her that.
She made me hustle though, getting her out of her dress.

K.   That so.   How was the cabin?

O.   Just like any cabin always is.

K.   Can it.   You know what I mean.   Was it all tidy, or did it
look as though she'd had a party there?

O.   If she'd had ten parties I wouldn't be telling you.   I like
Miss Ferri and I like my job.

K.   I get you.   Maybe you wouldn't object to a party yourself
some time?

        (NOTES CONCLUDED ON THIS AS HAVING NO FURTHER REFERENCE TO
            CASE.)

Police Department.
Form RL/2120/C.7.

<u>DETECTIVE OFFICER NEAME'S SHORTHAND NOTES OF DETECTIVE OFFICER</u>

<u>KETTERING'S SECOND EXAMINATION OF MR CARLTON ROCKSAVAGE.</u>

K.   Good morning, Mr. Rocksavage.

R.   'Morning, Mr. Kettering.

K.   What's the latest quotation for Argus Suds?

R.   Eh!   Oh, they opened at $13\frac{1}{2}$ this morning, but why the question?

K.   I was just thinking what a fine break it is for you that Blane should have faded out just when he did.

R.   What the devil d'you mean?

K.   Only that you must be picking up those Argus shares by the bucket full and making a fine thing out of it.   That's all, Mr. Rocksavage.

R.   Now look here, what are you insinuating?

K.   I'm not insinuating anything.   I'm only voicing what is quite apparent to anybody who knows anything of your financial situation during the past few weeks.   You were up against it Mr. Rocksavage.   Up against it pretty badly until Blane's death, but once that happened it was easy enough for you to get all the financial backing you needed and you're picking up Blane's shares as hard as you can go, so that before you're much older you'll have control of his companies as well as your own.   That will make you the unchallenged king of the soap market with a secure future.   It's a bit unfortunate though that Blane should have died on your yacht.

R.   Everything you say is perfectly true.   I admit that, as you would see it, I had a strong motive for putting Blane out of the way, but very fortunately the facts of the case place me absolutely beyond any suspicion.   I did not leave the lounge until ten past eight, so how could I possibly have murdered a man, disposed of his body, and changed for dinner - all in twenty minutes?

K.   Twenty-five, Mr. Rocksavage.   You didn't get back to the lounge until 8.35 and I hear you are an expert quick-change artist.   I've just been talking to Mr. Jocelyn.   He tells me that you wagered Count Posodini a hundred dollars that you would change in under 4 minutes on the night before Blane's death, and that you won your bet.   If you did that the night Blane died it would have left you a full 20 minutes to commit this crime and clear up afterwards.

R.   So Jocelyn said that did he, but wait a minute, how d'you know that he didn't do this job?   I passed him in the passage, still unchanged, at ten past eight, when I went down to change myself.

K.   Did you now!

R.   I did, so perhaps you'll exercise your talents in finding out what he was up to between 7.45 and 8.10.   There was much more time for him to have done this job than me.

K.   He hadn't got your motive.

R.   He certainly had.   He's always lived above his income. For the last five years he's been entirely dependent on Lady Welter.   She's in a jam because of those fool papers she runs.

She loses a packet on them every year, yet she won't give them up

because she just lives for this christian crusading business.

If I'd failed to do a deal with Blane she would have gone under

with me and young Jocelyn would have found himself on his uppers.

He stood to benefit just as much by Blane's death as I did.

More, in fact, because even if Rocksavage Consolidated had gone

down the drain I have other resources.

K.   I get your point, Mr. Rocksavage.

R.   How about the Jap too?

K.   How about him?

R.   Well, he stood in to lose a million dollars if Blane had

lived long enough to come to an arrangement with me.

K.   I'd certainly like to hear some more about that, Mr.

Rocksavage.

R.   It's this way. Officially he's acting for the Shikoku

people and he's been trying to sell me the Japanese soap monopoly

on their behalf for months past, but he's playing ball with

another crowd called the Totomi Soap Company on the side.

They're in a position where they might be able to queer the pitch

as a home producing firm by rousing national opinion against the

monopoly going outside Japan, unless they're squared first. Their

price was a million, so Hayashi wouldn't have got it all, but I'll

bet he stood in for a pretty useful split. I wouldn't conclude

though, once I got the idea of coming to terms with Blane, but if

my deal with him had fallen through Hayashi knew he could count on

my signing up. It's plain sailing for him now Blane's out of the way, and you know what these Orientals are. He had a mighty strong motive to do in Blane in order to prevent Blane and me getting together.

K.   That's certainly something to work on Mr. Rocksavage and I'll get down to following up what you've said of Jocelyn and Hayashi right away.

R.   Good.   And there's no trouble I won't go to in helping your investigation.   I don't need telling the sort of thing that people are going to say on account of Blane having died on my yacht, so its to my interest, more than anybody's, that poor Blane's murderer should be brought to book.

K.   Don't worry, Mr. Rocksavage, we'll get him.

DETECTIVE OFFICER NEAME'S SHORTHAND NOTES OF DETECTIVE OFFICER KETTERING'S SECOND EXAMINATION OF LADY WELTER.

K.   Come in, Lady Welter.   I hope you're feeling a little **more** reasonable this morning.   I've got to ask you a few more questions and the sooner you realise that rudeness and obstruction will only prolong the ordeal the better it will be for you.

L.W.   I find all this most tiresome. I've already told you that I know nothing whatsoever about this man Blane's death.

K.   It hasn't occurred to you I suppose that you might be charged with it?

L.W.   What! I! You're mad, my man. I shall report you.

K.   You can make any report you like but it won't alter the **fact** that you had a very strong motive for wishing Bolitho Blane out **of** the way.

L.W.   This is ridiculous.

K.   Not at all.   You lost a big portion of your fortune in 1929, you've been paying up the losses on these papers which **you** run for years and now you are up against it, because the Rock-savage companies in which the remainder of your money is inves**ted** passed their dividend last year.   Owing to Blane's death Rocksavage is back on his feet again and you with him.

L.W.   Well, if that is so Mr. Rocksavage benefits by this **man** Blane's death just as much as I do.

K.   You're wrong there.   Rocksavage has other assets outside his soap companies, whereas you haven't, so motive is stronger **in** your case.

L.W.   This is absurd, as though an elderly woman like myself **could** murder a man and push him out of the porthole.

K.   You're only 55 Lady Welter and a strong, well preserved woman at that.   Let me assure you from my police experience that many a woman with less physical strength than yourself could have done this business and in your case the motive was there. Moreover, there is no check on your movements from the time you came below with the Bishop at 7.5 until you arrived in the lounge changed at 8.5 on the night of Blane's death.

L.W.   Oh, yes there is, young man.   My maid was with me, helping me to dress for dinner.

K.   Ah, now that puts a very different complexion on it, but why didn't you tell me that before Lady Welter?

L.W.   Because I didn't think you could be such a fool as to suspect a woman like myself of a crime like this.

K.   Was she with you the whole time?

L.W.   No, I rang for her when I reached my cabin and she was with me for about half an hour, until I had finished dressing.

K.   Wait a moment then, that only gets us to about 7.35, and we know Blane was alive at 7.45.   You were already changed and you had twenty minutes, therefore, in which you might have done this job before arriving in the lounge.

L.W.   I was in my cabin the whole time.

K.   So you say Lady, but I want proof of that and, if you're a wise woman, you'll do your best to produce it.

L.W.   Proof!   But how can anybody prove such a thing.   You must take my word for it.

K.   I'm afraid I want something more than that.   What were
you doing all that time?

L.W.   Well, if you must know, I was knitting a jumper.   I only
had one sleeve to do so I thought I would finish it before I went
up to dinner.

K.   Can you give me any proof of that?

L.W.   Yes.   My maid knows just how far I had got with the
jumper before I dressed that evening and I left it finished on
the table for her to press when I left my cabin half an hour
later.

K.   Can you produce the jumper Lady Welter?

L.W.   Yes.

K.   All right.   That'll do for the moment .... no, not
out of that door.   D'you mind stepping into the next cabin for
a few moments.   I'm going to see your maid and I don't want
there to be any chance of your fixing things up between you
before I've had a word with her.

L.W.   What impertinence!

DETECTIVE OFFICER NEAME'S SHORTHAND NOTES OF DETECTIVE OFFICER
KETTERING'S EXAMINATION OF LADY WELTER'S MAID, MILDRED SHORT.

K.   Come in Mildred.   Just a few questions I want to ask you
about what happened on the night Mr. Blane met his death.

M.   Yes, sir.

K.   What time did Lady Welter ring for you to come along and
help her dress that night?

M.   I think it was about ten past seven, sir, that is when I
got to her ladyship's cabin.

K.   How long were you with her?

M.   Just under half an hour sir.   I was back in the service
room down below by twenty-five to eight.

K.   Lady Welter was busy knitting a jumper that day, wasn't she?

M.   Yes, sir.

K.   Do you remember how far she had got with it before she
sent for you to help her to dress?

M.   She only had one sleeve left to do sir.

K.   How long would that take her?

M.   About half an hour, sir.   It was only a short sleeve,
you see.

K.   When you came back to her cabin, after she had gone up,
did you notice if the jumper was just the same, or had she done
anything to it?

M.   I didn't see it then, sir.   In fact, I was wondering
yesterday what had happened to it because I haven't seen it since.

K.   Is that so?   All right.   You can go, Mildred.

DETECTIVE OFFICER NEAME'S SHORTHAND NOTES OF DETECTIVE OFFICER KETTERING'S SECOND EXAMINATION OF MR. INOSUKE HAYASHI.

K.   Good morning, Mr. Hayashi.

H.   Good morning, Officer.

K.   I don't think you were quite frank with me yesterday.

H.   Oh, but I am always frank.   I answer everything you ask - yes?

K.   Maybe, but you didn't go out of your way to give me any extra information, did you?   For instance, you didn't tell me that you had written a note to Blane asking him either to come to your cabin or give you a meeting in his before dinner.

H.   I did not think that had any bearing on the case.

K.   It has a bearing which may make things look very nasty for you, Mr. Hayashi.   What time did Blane come to your cabin?

H.   He did not come to my cabin.

K.   Then what time did you go to his?

H.   I did not go to his cabin.   Poor man, he ignored my note, perhaps because he had no option.

K.   What time did you send that postcard along to him?

H.   About ten past seven, soon after Mr. Blane came on board. I wrote it in the small writing-room here and sent it down at once.

K.   What were you so anxious to see him about?

H.   It is quite simple.   I have the disposal of the soap monopoly of my country in my hands.   I must get the best price for my country that I can.   I have been negotiating for its sale by correspondence with both Mr. Rocksavage and Mr. Blane, but neither would make me a definite offer.   I knew that if these two once got together the chances were that they would arrange an amalgamation.   That would have put an end to their competition and my government would have had to accept a much lesser price in consequence.   It was my business, therefore, to try and arrange a deal with one of these two gentlemen before they met.   I spoke to Mr. Rocksavage soon after I came on board in the afternoon, and he was unwilling to deal with me until he had seen Mr. Blane. His position was, of course, then far stronger than Mr. Blane's, because the shares of the Blane companies had been falling so heavily during the past few weeks.   In consequence, I determined to see Mr. Blane, if I could, and try to persuade him to make a firm deal with me.   If he had done so it would have strengthened his position in dealing with Mr. Rocksavage tremendously.   I do not know if you are well acquainted with the methods of finance but whichever of these gentlemen had purchased the monopoly I have to offer would have been able to float a new issue upon it and, thereby, draw much fresh capital, which they badly needed, into their concerns.   I hoped that Mr. Blane might have been persuaded to see the wisdom of saving himself in this manner, before he opened negotiations with Mr. Rocksavage.

K.   And what did you hope to gain for yourself, if you could have pulled the deal off?

H.   For myself, nothing.   I am only the employee of the Shikoku Products Company.

K.   So you say, but what were you standing in to make on the side?

H.   This suggestion you make is one which I resent most
strongly.

K.   Now you can cut out that high moral stuff right away, and
I'm warning you that you had best come clean.   Mr. Rocksavage has
given me the low down on the situation.   You'd have us believe
that you're trying to get the highest price you can for the
Shikoku people, who are acting for your government, but that is
not the case.   The thing you're interested in is the highest
bribe you can get to split with the Totomi Soap people, in order
to stall them off from wrecking the deal.   Rocksavage told me
himself that he had promised you $1,000,000 to split with them if
the deal went through.   It's my opinion that you were scared
that if Rocksavage and Blane got together they would no longer
be prepared to pay you enough to square the Totomi people, so the
whole thing would have fallen through.

H.   That I deny.

K.   Deny it if you like, but it's the truth and we can prove it.
In consequence it becomes quite plain now that you had the
strongest possible motives for getting rid of Blane.   If he and
Rocksavage had ever got together it looked as if you were going to
lose your share of a million dollars.

H.   Do I understand that you accuse me of the murder of this man
Blane?

K.   That's about what it looks like to me.

H.   No, no - please.   You make here a big mistake.   I have no hand in that - none whatever.

K.   Do you deny that Rocksavage had offered you a big bribe
which you intended to split with the Totomi Soap Company, and
that you feared you would lose it if Rocksavage and Blane came to
an understanding?

H.   On that question I give not my answer now.   I reserve it for
my defence, should you make the error to charge me with this crime.

K.   Unfortunately you are unable to prove any alibi.   You say
you went to your cabin at 6.10 and you did not arrive changed in
the lounge . . .

H.   But I came up again.   I wrote the postcard which you found
in Mr. Blane's cabin, here, in this writing room, between seven
and ten past.

K.   You might have mentioned that yesterday. What did you do then?

H.   I went down again.

K.   Well, that doesn't help us any as you were in your cabin
between 7.45 and 8.15 and during those thirty minutes, you may
have murdered Blane as I suggest.

H.   No, no.   I was in the cabin all that time.   Working,
please, on my papers and, wait, the steward can prove that I was
there at 7.50, because I rang for him.

K.   Why?

H.   To bring me some writing paper.   When I asked for it before
there was none, as the chief steward had only just returned from
Miami and he had the key of the store where it was locked up.
That was why I wrote first on a postcard.   The steward came back

with the writing paper about five minutes after I asked him for it.

K.   Were you changed then?

H.   No, I had not then changed.   I was still in lounge suit at five to eight.   The steward can prove that.   How then could I change my clothes and murder a man in the short space of 20 minutes when, in that time, I also wrote a longish letter?

K.   Where is that letter?

H.   I see no reason why I should answer that question.   The document is a secret one and can add nothing to your investigations.

K.   Mr. Hayashi, you don't seem to realise that you are under suspicion of having committed murder.   It is vital for your own sake that you should produce any evidence that will free you from suspicion.

H.   It may be true that I am under suspicion, but I hope sincerely, Detective Officer, that you will not do anything so foolish as to charge me with murder.   I have assured you that that letter exists.   It could be produced, and if produced it would clear me of suspicion immediately.   It would also, er .....
make rather a fool of you, so I pray you do not force me to produce it.

K.   Aw, these Oriental tricks won't wash with me.   If you'd been writing a letter during those twenty minutes you'd only be too pleased to fetch it up.   Will you or won't you?

H.   I have nothing more to say to you, Sir.

K.   O.K.   I've done my best for you.

DETECTIVE OFFICER NEAME'S SHORTHAND NOTES OF DETECTIVE OFFICER KETTERING'S SECOND EXAMINATION OF THE BISHOP OF BUDE.

K.   Good morning, Bishop.   I hope you're feeling all right again now.   That was a rotten business your throwing a faint on us yesterday.

B.   Thank you, thank you, I am better, yes; but my heart you know has been troubling me for some little time and I'm rather subject to these sudden attacks.

K.   Now, that's real bad, particularly as I've got to ask you some rather unpleasant questions.

B.   Dear, dear, I cannot think what they would be about. I have nothing to hide, nothing at all, I assure you.

K.   Well, I hope that is so for all our sakes, but I want the truth about your relations with Bolitho Blane.

B.   A casual acquaintance made years ago.   I barely knew the man, as I told you yesterday.

K.   Now, that won't do. You evidently haven't looked in your black despatch box this morning, or you'd realise that, when I was searching the cabins yesterday, I removed that letter from it Blane wrote you a few days back from the Adlon-Claridge in New York.   In that he spoke of the wonderful friendship you had for each other.

B.   Oh, er - that.   What an extraordinary letter it was, wasn't it?   I took it to be some kind of a joke.   I could hardly regard it as anything else, but I did remember from my meeting with him in the past that Blane had a very queer sense of humour - very queer.

K.   Pointless sort of joke, wasn't it?

B.   Quite pointless, but we all know now that the poor fellow
was half off his head with worry.   I imagine he must have been
suffering from some strange reaction caused by overstrain when
he wrote it.   Those protestations of friendship were so absurd
when you consider that I had only met the man quite casually.

K.   I don't consider anything of the kind, Bishop.   In 1917
you knew Blane mighty well.

B.   What - what's that?

K.   You heard.   You remember that nasty business in 1917,
so nasty that we just won't talk about it.   You were in that
up to the neck and Blane knew it.   For reasons we needn't go
into, he decided not to spill the beans at the time, and so you
managed to get away with it.   If you hadn't you wouldn't be a
bishop to-day, but Blane hadn't forgotten he had the goods on
you and, when he contemplated doing some funny business during
his trip in this yacht, he took the precaution of writing you
first to tip you off that if you didn't keep your mouth shut
he meant to put you through the hoop.   Now, what have you got
to say?

B.   I protest, sir.   I protest.   An Episcopal Court
exonerated me completely - on every charge - in that most
unsavoury matter in which it was my ill-fortune to be involved
when I was with the troops in 1917.

K.   An Episcopal Court might have preferred to give you the benefit of the doubt rather than have a prominent churchman involved in a public scandal.

B.   Be careful, sir.   There is, I warn you, such a thing as the law of libel.

K.   I should worry.   You wouldn't dare to rake that unsavoury scandal up by bringing an action in a civil court but, unless you're very careful, it's all going to come out now whether you want it to or no.

B.   What d'you mean?   You don't think I - I ....

K.   Well maybe we won't have to rake it up, but that largely depends on you.   It's my duty to get the man who has murdered Bolitho Blane and, if you'll give me your assistance, I'll do my best to keep you out of this business as far as I can.

B.   That's very kind - very kind, indeed.   Of course you must quite understand, officer, that there was no foundation for those charges, none at all, but naturally I should find it most distressing to have that horrible affair made public after all these years.   I am afraid I don't see, though, how I can help you more than I have done already.

K.   You came below to your cabin at 7.5 on the night of Blane's death and you did not appear in the lounge until 8.5.   What were you doing all that time?   I want the truth now.

B.   I was in my cabin.   I never left it I assure you.

K.   Can you give me any proof that was so?

B.   No.   I fear that I cannot.

K.   I wonder if you realise the seriousness of your situation

Bishop.   Here is this man, Blane, who knew something which he might have published to your detriment.   He writes you a letter from New York containing a veiled threat that in certain circumstances he may give you away.   The moment he comes on board you go down to your cabin.   If you had started to change then you had forty clear minutes in which to do so, which would bring you round to 7.45, and then fifteen clear minutes before you appeared in the lounge to kill that man who was holding a threat over you.   You were the only person on board who had ever met Blane before and you had a very strong motive for wishing him out of the way.   D'you understand now how black this case looks against you?

B.   But surely you're not suggesting that - that ....

K.   I certainly am.

B.   But my dear sir, this is - well really!

K.   It's really a very strong case against you, unless you can prove what you were doing between 7.5 and 8.0.

B.   Nothing, absolutely nothing, except changing in my cabin. I give you my word but, unfortunately, there is no way in which I can prove it.

K.   All right, then, but I'm afraid I shall have to talk to you again later on.

DETECTIVE OFFICER KETTERING'S FOURTH REPORT, CONTINUED.

Having re-examined all the parties, I proceeded to a new analysis of the situation and composed a fresh draft of possible motives.

POSSIBLE MOTIVES (No. 2.)   10.3.36.

Mrs. Jocelyn.   Nil, as far as is known at the moment, but she is in collusion with her husband, supporting his statement that he was in his bath at 7.45, when we know that he was not, and she may or may not have been in her own cabin at that hour.

Count Posodini Alias "Slick" Daniels.   A motive, in that he admits that it was through Blane's agency that he was sent down for his first term in Sing Sing, and that Jocelyn brought him on board with the deliberate intention of giving him the opportunity of getting even with Blane.   It is even possible that Jocelyn may have paid him to do the job, or that they did the job between them.   His alibi depends on his being able to prove that Mrs. Jocelyn was in his cabin from 7.45 till 8.10, and this she denies.

Mr. Rocksavage.   Strong motive, and it is now proved, owing to his capability of changing in under four minutes, that he had ample time to commit the crime between 8.10 and 8.30.

The Bishop of Bude.   Strong motive.   In the Bishop's previous statement he said that he had only met Blane casually in an English country house once about seven years ago (1929), whereas he does not now deny that he met Blane in France in 1917.   Blane's letter shows that there was some strong tie up between the two.   It now seems certain that this was in connection with the unsavoury business that the Bishop is so anxious should not be made public.   The probability is that Blane was holding this over him and, as there was ample opportunity for the Bishop to commit the crime, he now comes strongly under suspicion.

Lady Welter.   Strong motive, owing to the fact that it looks as though she would have been completely bankrupt if the Rocksavage companies had gone under and no longer in a position to finance the group of papers which are her principal life interest.

Mr. Hayashi.   Strong motive.   It now appears that he stood to lose a considerable sum of money if Blane and Rocksavage had ever got together.

Mr. Jocelyn.   Strong motive.   Lady Welter's bankruptcy would have thrown him back into the precarious existence which he was leading between 1923 and 1931, with the additional burden of a wife to support.   It is now proved that he told a direct lie in his early statement where he said that he was in his bath at 7.45, since Mr. Rocksavage met him in the passage still unchanged at 8.10.   Moreover, "Slick" Daniels' evidence goes to show that Jocelyn had deliberately invited him on board in the hope that he might square accounts with Blane.

Miss Rocksavage.   Nil, as far as is known at the moment.

DETECTIVE OFFICER KETTERING'S FOURTH REPORT,   CONTINUED.

The foregoing examinations and the writing of the report have occupied me all morning and at the moment I admit that I am completely baffled.   Only the two stewards, the ship's carpenter and Stodart are conclusively ruled out, it having been quite impossible for any of them, or any other member of the crew to commit this crime.

Against Miss Rocksavage and the Hon. Mrs. Jocelyn we have no evidence of motive, although both of them had opportunity.

On the other hand there was motive and, in many cases, very strong motive against Count Posodini, Mr. Rocksavage, the Bishop of Bude, Lady Welter, Mr. Hayashi and the Hon. Reginald Jocelyn; and all of these had opportunity.

A further report will follow this evening.

Keys Kettering

Detective Officer

Florida Police.

1.35 p.m.   10.3.36.   on S.Y. Golden Gull.

Police Department.
Form RL/2120/C.7.

DETECTIVE OFFICER KETTERING'S FIFTH REPORT.

After lunch to-day Mr. Rocksavage came to me and said that he would like to see me privately. We went to the small writing room together and he told me that our interview of the morning had greatly upset him. He again protested his complete innocence of Blane's death and said that, in spite of any unpleasantness which might arise for him out of the matter, he had decided to inform me of certain facts which would clear him altogether. He then sent for Doctor Ackland, his personal doctor, who always travels with him, and in the presence of the doctor, Detective Officer Neame and myself, he made the following voluntary statement.

This statement has been duly vouched for as the truth and signed and witnessed by Dr. Ackland.

VOLUNTARY STATEMENT MADE BY MR. CARLTON ROCKSAVAGE.   10.3.36.

As a man who is responsible for many millions of other peoples' money, I have been subject to bouts of acute worry at times, when my affairs have not been going well.   In consequence, a few years ago, I took to the habit of administering drugs to myself by injection; their purpose being not to allay nerves but to key me up for further efforts at times when I was suffering from severe strain.

Dr. Ackland has always prepared these injections for me and, on the night in question, I brought him down to my cabin with me for this purpose, as I anticipated having to enter into a strenuous conference with Blane that night after dinner.   It was customary for me to rest for a quarter of an hour after the injection, in order that the drug might take effect.   I did so on this occasion.   Dr. Ackland remained with me until I had changed and went up to the lounge for dinner.

I could have mentioned the doctor's presence before as an alibi and given some false cause for his presence in my cabin but, in view of this police investigation, where my habit of injecting myself with drugs might come to light later, I felt that suspicion might be cast upon Dr. Ackland's veracity unless I told the whole truth now.

Carlton Rocksavage.

The foregoing statement was written in my presence and I bear witness to its entire truth.

Frank C. Ackland Ph S.D. F.C.S.R.

HAIR FOUND IN MISS FERRI ROCKSAVAGE'S COMB ON THE MORNING OF

9.3.36.

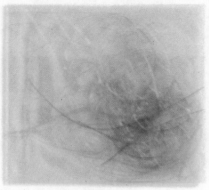

MATCH FOUND IN THE BISHOP OF BUDE'S CABIN ON THE MORNING OF

9.3.36.

PHOTOGRAPH OF 6 CIGARETTE ENDS (ALL PLAYER'S) FOUND IN COUNT

POSODINI'S CABIN ON THE MORNING OF 9.3.36.

DETECTIVE OFFICER NEAME'S SHORTHAND NOTES OF DETECTIVE OFFICER KETTERING'S EXAMINATION OF DOCTOR FRANK ACKLAND, Ph.S.D., F.C.S.B.

K.   Doctor, you have just vouched for this statement of Mr. Rocksavage, that you went below with him at 8.10.   You are quite certain that is correct?

A.   Yes.

K.   But you weren't in the lounge with him?

A.   No.   I was sitting just outside, enjoying the evening air on deck.   As Mr. Rocksavage passed the deck entrance of the lounge he saw me and beckoned.   I knew at once what he wanted, so I got up without a word and followed him down.

K.   You had to come into the lounge to follow him down the companion-way though.

A.   Yes.   A few steps, that's all, as the companion-way is within a couple of yards of the deck entrance.

K.   No one in the lounge seems to have noticed you.   Don't you think that strange?

A.   No.   The Bishop, Lady Welter and Mr. Stodart were sitting together at a table with their backs to the companion-way and the deck entrance, so they would not have been likely to notice me as I stepped through.   Cane, the lounge steward, saw me though. Ask him if you doubt my word, and Mr. Jocelyn too.   Mr. Rocksavage and I passed him in the passage way below.

K.   Thanks, doctor.   If the lounge steward saw you I guess that will do.

Police Department.

Form RL/2120/C.7.

DETECTIVE OFFICER KETTERING'S FIFTH REPORT, CONTINUED.

I then examined the contents of the wastepaper baskets, which had been removed from each of the parties' cabins on the morning following the crime, and three items of interest emerged from this examination.

In the refuse from Count Posodini's cabin I found 31 cigarette ends, 25 of these are Chesterfields, but the other 6 are an English brand called Players, and four out of these six have obvious traces of lipstick on them.

In the refuse from Miss Rocksavage's cabin I found a twist of hair which had obviously been removed from a comb.   Most of this was golden hair, which undoubtedly comes from the head of Miss Ferri Rocksavage, but mingled with it there are a few short, black curly hairs, which definitely suggest that a man had used that comb after her.

Among the refuse from the Bishop of Bude's cabin I found one match torn out of a booklet of matches, upon which is printed in block letters the words "Adlon-Claridge."

I then re-examined various members of the party.

DETECTIVE OFFICER NEAME'S SHORTHAND NOTES OF DETECTIVE OFFICER KETTERING'S THIRD EXAMINATION OF THE HONOURABLE MRS. JOCELYN.

K.   Come in, Mrs. Jocelyn.   Sit down, do.

P.J.   What, more questions, already?

K.   Yes.   Sorry I've got to trouble you again, but let's make it as pleasant as we can.   Have a cigarette?

P.J.   No thanks, I only smoke my own.

K.   Right then.   May I have one of yours so we can be sociable?

P.J.   Certainly.

K.   I see you smoke Players.   Very popular brand in England?

P.J.   Very.

K.   That's a charming shade of lipstick you use Mrs. Jocelyn.

P.J.   Need we go into that?

K.   I'm afraid we've got to.   I'm going to trouble you for the lipstick you have in your bag at the moment.

P.J.   But - I don't understand.

K.   Never mind.   Just hand it over, will you.   It'll save all sorts of trouble in the end if you'll oblige me now.

P.J.   All right.   There's nothing very exciting about my lipstick, but I'm sure I don't want to be searched.   Here it is.

K.   Thanks.   You won't mind if I keep it will you?   We shall need it later to prove that it matches the lipstick on these cigarette ends which I've got in this little tin box - see?

P.J.   Why - yes.   But ....

K.   Players, all of them, Mrs. Jocelyn, smoked by you and found the morning after Blane's death in Count Posodini's cabin.   Now,

don't get me all wrong.   I'm not trying to fix you for murder,
and I'm not trying to raise any nasty scandal about you.   The
point is that some time between the morning of the 8th and the
morning of the 9th you smoked these cigarettes in Posodini's
cabin.   If it was, as I have reason to believe, between 7.45 and
8.10 p.m. that lets you out of any suggestion that you were doing
anything with the Count that you shouldn't have, because it's not
reasonable to suppose that you would have smoked six cigarettes
and had much of a necking party in a matter of twenty-five
minutes.   On the other hand, if you didn't smoke them at that
time, it might suggest that you were there for a very much longer
period and then - no offence - but it might be suggested that you
and the Count were up to the sort of thing your husband wouldn't
care to hear about.

P.J.   I have nothing to add to my previous statement.

K.   All right, Mrs. Jocelyn.   Then the presumption is that you
were in the Count's cabin at some other, and probably a much
longer, period during that twenty-four hours.   If that comes out,
as it may quite well have to in a case like this, what will your
husband have to say?

P.J.   A lot I expect.

K.   That doesn't appear to worry you over much?

P.J.   As a matter of fact it's just the sort of little lesson I've
been meaning to give him for some time.

K.   So he's been playing you up with Ferri, eh?   I guessed as
much.

P.J.   I did not say so.

K.   Wait a minute, though.   I'm going to put you wise to something which may make you think differently before you burn your boats.   The bird you know as Count Posodini is actually "Slick" Daniels; con man and card sharp.   Here's his police record.   Take a look.   Now, what about it when the press get hold of that?   Can't you see the headlines in the news sheets. "Society dame becomes moll of well-known crook."   That's not going to be so funny for you, is it?   You'll sure be ruined socially and that's a high price to pay just to get your own back on your husband.

P.J.   Yes - yes, it would be horrible.

K.   All right, then, why not tell me the truth.

P.J.   I have nothing to add to my previous statement.

K.   Oh Lordy!   Let me put it to you another way, then.   Mr. Rocksavage and the ship's doctor both saw your husband still unchanged in the passage at 8.10.   So your bluff about his being in his bath at 7.45 is now quite useless.   Get that?

P.J.   Yes.

K.   On the other hand there is very strong presumptive evidence that Posodini did in Blane.   As "Slick" is a known criminal that makes the presumption doubly strong.   Now, you seem a decent sort of girl.   Just because a man has a criminal record behind him you're surely not going to see him sent to the chair for a murder he didn't do, if you can stop it, are you?

P.J.   I see.   Yes, that does make a big difference, doesn't it?

All right, then, I was in the Count's cabin.   When we came below at a quarter to eight I went in to borrow a book and I sat there talking to him for the best part of half an hour.

K.   Then, why the heck didn't you say so to begin with?

P.J.   Isn't that obvious?

K.   Yes, because your husband told you not to.   Did he know where you'd been?

P.J.   I intended that he should.   I suppose I might as well tell you everything now.   My husband and I haven't been getting on very well lately and this trip has brought matters to a head.   I don't worry much about his having an occasional affair, because he's the type of man who's never quite grown up, and it seems that sort of thing is absolutely necessary to him.   You see I try to persuade myself that he never really goes off the rails, but this business with Ferri Rocksavage has been a bit too much.   I jib at being made a fool of in public and, of course, he considers that I'm as safe as houses, because I'm very very fond of him and I've never looked at another man.   I thought that it might bring him to his senses if I did, so when he and Ferri started throwing eyes at each other on the first day out from New York I decided to start a party of my own with the Count.   I knew quite well that I could take care of myself and I thought that, if I spent half an hour alone with the Count in his cabin, before changing that night, Reggie would be certain to ask why I was so late.   As it was I had all my trouble for nothing.   He was so occupied himself that he never even thought to ask where I had been.

K.   I understand.

P.J.   I wouldn't have told you this unless you'd had proof already
that he didn't come down till ten past eight, but now, as there's
no object in keeping up my original story, at least I can get the
Count out of trouble.   I'm glad to do that because, whether he's
a gaolbird or not, he's a very amusing and kindhearted person.

K.   Thank you, Mrs. Jocelyn.   I really am grateful to you for
having cleared this matter up.

DETECTIVE OFFICER KETTERING'S FIFTH REPORT, CONTINUED.

The Hon. Mrs. Jocelyn had only just left when Lady Welter's maid, Mildred Short, appeared at the door of the writing room and asked if she might have a word with me.   She was very nervous, but, after a little, I got her to tell me her trouble and, from a big work bag which she was carrying, she produced a pale blue knitted jumper.   In the middle of the back of the jumper there was a large burn where it had been singed with a hot iron and, after some persuasion, Mildred Short made the following statement about it.

VOLUNTARY STATEMENT BY MILDRED SHORT.   10.3.36.

As previously stated, when I went to Lady Welter's cabin at about 7.10, this jumper still lacked one sleeve.   When I returned to her ladyship's cabin to tidy it at 8.30, the jumper was lying on the table finished, and I knew that her ladyship had left it there for me to take below and press.   Later that evening I proceeded to do so but I was called away and, most unfortunately, left the electric iron on it.   This resulted in a large burn in the middle of the back which I could not possibly disguise, and I became most desperately worried in consequence.

Her ladyship is a good mistress, but hard.   She has a terrible tongue when she's angry and I was scared out of my wits as to what she would say to me about ruining her jumper, seeing that she had knitted it herself.   In my fright I decided to say nothing and, if she asked me about it later on, pretend that it had got lost.   With all the to do about the murder on the following day her ladyship never said anything about the jumper and I was beginning to hope that she had forgotten all about it, until she sent for me and questioned me this morning.

At first I protested that the jumper had got lost somewhere, but when her ladyship impressed upon me how important it was that its whereabouts should be discovered I broke down and told her the truth.   She said I must tell you exactly what had happened and that is the truth as God is my witness.

Mildred Short

Witnessed: *Kays Kettering*

Detective Officer, Florida Police.
1256, Palm Avenue.

DETECTIVE OFFICER NEAME'S SHORTHAND NOTES OF DETECTIVE OFFICER

KETTERING'S THIRD EXAMINATION OF MISS FERRI ROCKSAVAGE.

K.   Sorry to bother you again, Miss Rocksavage.   Come and sit down, won't you.

F.R.   Well?

K.   Look here, help me out will you.

F.R.   I always help people out if I can.

K.   That's a good girl.   You got a sunny nature, haven't you? You're always being nice to people, whether they deserve it or not.

F.R.   Oh, I don't know about that, but it's a short life and it's no good being miserable.

K.   You've said it, and that's why I'm hoping you're not going to blow up on what I'm going to say.

F.R.   Why should I?

K.   Well, I don't know, you're a young girl.   Very well brought up and that sort of thing.   Some girls like that might resent the sort of questions I'm going to ask, but you know I wouldn't do it if I didn't have to in the course of my duty.   Now, I'm going to treat you just as though you weren't a young society girl at all. I'm going to talk to you as though you were a woman of the world.

F.R.   I suppose I am what you call a woman of the world.   Most girls are these days.

K.   That's right.   Now, I'm sure you don't want any sort of scandal attached to your name and believe me a scandal is the last thing that I want to involve you in, but there's one thing I've

got to ask you.   Who was the man who was in your cabin on the
night that Blane met his death?

F.R.   I don't understand.

K.   Oh, yes you do, and you can take it from me that I have
actual proof that a man was there.   You can take your choice:
come clean with me now or face it out against the evidence that I
shall produce when you're in the witness box, with all the press
photographers standing round to take shots of you at forty
different angles.   Who was the man in your cabin the night that
Blane met his death?

F.R.   You're bluffing.   You haven't got any evidence.

K.   Yes I have.   Take a look at this little bunch of hair.
That came out of your comb.   It was found in the wastepaper
basket the night after Blane was murdered.   The fair hair's **yours**
but the short dark curly hairs are not.   Somebody used this comb
to tidy their hair after you had ruffled it, before leaving your
cabin.   Those strands of yours were probably already in it at **the**
time.   Anyhow, you'd have cleaned it before you used it to do
your hair when you dressed for dinner.   Shall I tell you who
those dark hairs belong to?

F.R.   Who?

K.   Reggie Jocelyn.

F.R.   Very ingenious, Mr. Van Dine, but we had a swim off the
yacht earlier in the afternoon.   I lent my comb to Mr. Jocelyn
then, after I'd used it and, being a lazy person, I suppose I
never thought to clean it afterwards.   Doesn't that rather upset

your clever little story?

K.   It might, Miss Rocksavage, if it weren't for the fact that a
man's life hangs in the balance.

F.R.   What d'you mean by that?

K.   Just this.   Reggie Jocelyn had a very strong motive for
wishing Bolitho Blane out of the way.   He even brought Count
Posodini on board, knowing the Count to be a criminal, with a
grudge against Blane.

F.R.   What!   Our handsome Count turns out to be a crook!

K.   That's so, and Jocelyn brought him on this trip in the hope
that he'd do Blane in.   He didn't, though.   Posodini's proved an
alibi and that makes the presumptive evidence even stronger
against your boy friend.   He swears that he was in his bath at
7.45, but his wife now admits that he wasn't.   What's more, he
was actually seen in the passage way still unchanged at ten past
eight.   Now, what was he doing between 7.45 and 8.10?   If he was
with you I think you'd better say so, because, if he wasn't, it
looks to me very much as though Jocelyn is going to stand his
trial for murder.

F.R.   In that case you win.   Reggie was with me, from the time
we came below, which was really about a quarter past seven, until
he left me at ten after eight.   I'm afraid that would hurt Mrs.
Jocelyn a lot if she knew, and father wouldn't be too pleased,
either.   Will you try and keep that out of it if you can?

K.   I'll do my best, Miss Rocksavage.   You're just paying the
penalty of being over kind to a good-looking young rascal, but I'm
prepared to take a little risk on being kind to you.

DETECTIVE OFFICER KETTERING'S FIFTH REPORT, CONTINUED.

After my third examination of Miss Ferri Rocksavage it occurred to me that the letter Hayashi alleged he had been writing might have been posted and would then still be in the postbag as, in the course of routine, I had given instructions on the morning of the 9th that no letters were to be sent ashore. This turned out to be the case, and I had the letter translated by the yacht's second cook, who is a Japanese. He attests that the original could not have been written in less than eight minutes, leaving Hayashi only twelve minutes to change. His story, therefore, appears to be true.

The lounge steward, Cane, confirms the fact that the supply of ship's notepaper in the writing room ran out early in the afternoon, before Hayashi came on board, and that he could not refill the racks until the chief steward, who had the keys of the store room, got back from his trip ashore. He further states that Hayashi handed him the letter for posting on arriving in the lounge at 8.15. It is obvious, therefore, that Hayashi could not have procured the paper earlier or written the letter at any other time than that appearing in his statement.

The cabin steward, Ringbottom, also confirms that Hayashi was still unchanged when he brought him the supply of ship's notepaper at 7.55.

Letter and attested translation herewith.

拝啓

陳者　四國に対しロックサベダ氏或はブローン氏の何れかと取引を

為すべき指令の如く承はる事を通知申上ル

四國は貴殿に対し何故とも標傳するを拒絶せられ　文政

若し貴殿の云ふ傳る賠償金ありと世し小生の同等にて支傳

はざるべからず　米はブローン氏或はロックサベダ氏より支傳はる

手数料の如何に依るのに小

ロックサベダは一百万弗の貸金に同意する模様にて小生

の分前にて一万弗を予期せられ之は貴殿の受

け合ひしらる、最低頼らんと彼等に申置ル

高小生の費用をし此等に達せられ候はば比較を秋等

の間すて今配する事を提議する所存に指之、二の諒解

のルとに小生同件上取進むる可シ

敬具

林　伊三助

鹿島殿

S.Y. Golden Gull,

At sea 8.4.36.

My dear Kashima,

As you know instructions were given by Shikoku to do the business either with Mr. Rocksavage or with Mr. Blane.   Shikoku refused to offer you anything.   Therefore any compensation you may receive will have to come out of my own money.   It depends on the fee which will be paid to me by Mr. Blane or Mr. Rocksavage.

I understand that Rocksavage will agree to a loan of ten million dollars, and I may expect one million dollars for my share.   I told them that this was the lowest you would accept.

My expenses have been considerable, and I am therefore suggesting that we divide this amount between us, and on that understanding I am proceeding with the matter.

Yours

(Signed)   INOSUKE HAYASHI.

To the best of my knowledge and belief the above is a full and true translation of the letter handed to me by Detective Officer Kettering.

Jimmu Yamato

Ship's Cook.

Witnessed:

10.4.36.

Kays Kettering

Detective Officer

Florida Police.

<u>DETECTIVE OFFICER NEAME'S SHORTHAND NOTES OF DETECTIVE OFFICER</u>

<u>KETTERING'S THIRD EXAMINATION OF THE BISHOP OF BUDE.</u>

K.   Come in, Bishop.   Have you thought of anything since this morning which might show us how you were occupying yourself between 7.5 and 8.0 on the night of Blane's death?

B.   No.   I wish I could, but I can't think of anything.

K.   What time did Blane come to your cabin?

B.   Blane?

K.   Yes, Blane.   It's no good denying it.   I've got the goods on you.   Just a little thing that happened to be in your waste-paper basket.   See, it's a book match with "Adlon-Claridge" on it, the New York Hotel from which Blane wrote you a few days back. Nobody except Blane could have left it where we found it, and it proves that, after he came on board, he went along to see you in your cabin.   Now, what have you got to say?

B.   But Officer - I - I-

K.   I want the truth.   What time did Blane come along to you?

B.   Oh dear, oh dear.   This is terrible.   Quite terrible.

K.   What time did he come I say?

B.   Only a few minutes after the ship sailed.   I hadn't been in my cabin more than three minutes when he came in.

K.   How long did he stay?

B.   Only two minutes.   No more, I assure you.

K.   Why did he come?

E.   Just to ask if I had got his letter.

K.   What did he say?

B.   Only - only - after asking if I'd got his letter, that it would be well for me to remember that we were very very good friends indeed.

K.   Then you went back with him to his cabin?

B.   No.   No.

K.   You're prepared to swear to that?

B.   I am.

K.   That he left you at about 7.10 and you never saw him again?

B.   I - never - saw him again.

K.   Then what in hades were you doing all that time?   It didn't take you 50 minutes to change.

B.   No, no.   I read a little first, I told you, but I never left my cabin.   I am prepared to swear to that before Almighty God.

K.   What did you read?

B.   I read an essay of R. L. Stevenson's.

K.   What was it about?

B.   What was it about?   Why, it was ....well, you know I really can't remember; most odd indeed, I can't remember, most unusual.

K.   Listen Bishop, you're in a spot, you're in a spot I say. I've got all the movements of every other party in this ship checked up, and, unless you can prove your alibi, I am proposing to run you for the murder of Bolitho Blane.

B.   You can't, you can't do that.   I didn't do it.

K.   You had motive, you had opportunity.   You killed Bolitho

Blane and I'm sending you to the chair for it.   Get that.

B.   What was the essay about?   What was it about.   I don't

know; that infernal hammering all the time ....I couldn't

concentrate for a moment.

K.   What hammering ?   You haven't mentioned hammering before.

B.   Oh, indeed, it was terrible.   From about ten minutes after

Blane had left me until I went up to the lounge changed it didn't

stop for a moment.

K.   For the love of Mike!   Couldn't you have told me that

before?

B.   Why certainly, but I never thought it important.   Now what

was that essay about ?   I really ....

K.   Oh, to hell with the essay.   That hammering must have been

the carpenter who was outside your cabin all the time.

B.   Yes - yes, the carpenter.   I said good evening to him when

I went up to dinner at eight o'clock.

K.   Well, now, if that isn't the limit.   I'll check up on it,

but Bishop, I reckon it lets you out.

DETECTIVE OFFICER KETTERING'S FIFTH REPORT, CONTINUED.

In closing this report I now have to confess myself completely at a loss. The situation has developed this afternoon in a most remarkable manner and it is even more baffling than it was at mid-day.

After the examination which I conducted this morning it was quite apparent that numerous members of the party had ample motive for wishing Blane dead. The trouble appeared then to be to fix upon the actual perpetrator of the crime but, since then, so much new evidence has come to light I am now far more befogged than I was before.

In the last stages of my examination this afternoon I had quite made up my mind that the Bishop of Bude was the guilty party, but the ship's carpenter, Jenks, confirmed his statement and it is quite clear that he never left his cabin between 7.45 and 8.0, when he went straight up to the lounge.

The following is an analysis of what occurred according to my latest information, and in my opinion it would have been impossible to commit the murder, dispose of the body, and partially remove the bloodstains from the carpet in less than ten minutes.

Mrs. Jocelyn.   Could not have done it, because she was with "Slick" Daniels, Alias Count Posodini, from 7.45 till 8.10 in his cabin, and from 8.10 till 8.30 she was with her husband, changing.

Count Posodini, alias "Slick" Daniels.   Could not have done it, because he was in his cabin with Mrs. Jocelyn from 7.45 till 8.10, and from that time until 8.25, when he appeared in the lounge, he would have been occupied in changing.

Mr. Rocksavage.   Could not have done it, because from 8.10 when he came down to his cabin, until he went up changed at 8.35, Doctor Ackland was with him and vouches for his presence there.

The Bishop of Bude.   Could not have done it, because from 7.15 until 8.0 the ship's carpenter was doing a job of work outside his cabin and vouches for the fact that he never left it during the whole of that time.

Lady Welter.   Could not have done it, because her maid, Mildred Short was with her, in her cabin from 7.5 until 7.35, and from 7.35 till 8.5 she is proved to have been knitting the last sleeve of a jumper, which would have occupied her the whole of that time, until she went up to the lounge.

Mr. Hayashi.   Could not have done it, because, when he rang his bell at 7.50, the steward found him in his cabin still unchanged, and he was still unchanged when the steward returned at 7.55, with the notepaper.   Eight out of the following twenty minutes he was occupied in writing a letter and the balance in changing to arrive in the lounge at 8.15.

Mr. Jocelyn.   Could not have done it, because from 7.15, when he went below, he was with Miss Ferri Rocksavage in her cabin, until 8.10, and from that time until 8.30 he was with his wife changing.

Miss Rocksavage.   Could not have done it, because from 7.15

she was with Jocelyn in her cabin until 8.10, and from thence onwards she was occupied with changing in the presence of her maid, Nellie Orde.

It seems to me, therefore, that all the parties under suspicion have incontestable alibis and as we know that Stodart was in the company of various persons in the lounge from 7.30 until 8.33 he could not possibly have committed this murder either. Moreover it could not, on the evidence shown, have been any member of the crew. This leaves me at a completely dead end, and I am now awaiting further instructions.

Kays Kettering

Detective Officer
Florida Police.

4.55 p.m.   10.3.36.   on S.Y. Golden Gull.

DO NOT BREAK THIS STRIP UNTIL YOU HAVE
DECIDED, ON THE EVIDENCE SUBMITTED,
WHO MURDERED BOLITHO BLANE.

Police Department,
Form GO/7431/N 58

POLICE HEADQUARTERS,

MIAMI,

FLA.

5.50 p.m.   10.3.36.

MEMO.

To Detective Officer Kettering.

Solution of murder perfectly clear on evidence
submitted.

Arrest Bolitho Blane, now posing as his secretary,
for the murder of Nicholas Stodart.

John Milton Schwab.

Lieutenant
Florida Police.

LIEUTENANT SCHWAB'S ANALYSIS OF THE FOREGOING EVIDENCE.

The time of the murder was set between 7.45 and 8.30, owing to a message, supposedly in the victim's handwriting, appearing on a leaf torn from Stodart's diary which was not in existence until 7.40.

Compare the share quotations supposedly written by Stodart, however, with other examples of handwriting known to have been written by Blane. The word "Rocksavage" in the share list also occurs twice in Blane's letter to Stodart and twice in his letter to the Bishop. The similarity of the first to the other four immediately springs to the eye, only the "s" and the "g" differing to any extent. Other similarities appear on closer inspection and there can be no doubt that all three documents were written by the same person.

Not the victim, but the writer of the share quotations therefore wrote the alleged last message, so that there is no evidence as to when the murder was committed. The alibi of the man presumed to be Stodart begins only at 7.25 when he entered the lounge. If the crime was committed before that his alibi falls to the ground.

Examination of the evidence brings other points to light showing that the man known as Stodart throughout the investigation is in reality Bolitho Blane. These are as follows:

1.   Photograph D. of Blane's bathroom shows a safety razor on the washstand, whereas photograph E of Stodart's cabin shows a cut-throat razor on the washstand. The photograph presumed to be of Stodart, flashed by Detective Officer Neame on the morning

after the crime, shows a razor cut on the man's face. It is
obvious that he had always been used to shaving with a safety
razor but, as suite C was locked up after the murder, he could not
get at this, and had to do the best he could to shave himself with
the cut-throat razor that was in Stodart's cabin.

2.   On examination of the photograph presumed to be of Stodart,
it is apparent that the coat he is wearing is too big for him, as
the sleeve is over long, and the garment must have been built for
a slightly taller man.   It is obvious that Blane, having changed
identities with his secretary, had to wear his secretary's clothes
which did not quite fit him.

3.   It will be recalled that on the night of the 9th, when the
man presumed to be Stodart dined with Kettering, he complained of
an abscess which was causing him trouble with his false teeth and,
as the upper set were slipping badly, he was unable to eat any
solids.   An examination of photograph D of Blane's bathroom,
shows a tooth brush and a plate brush, the latter being an
indication that Blane had false teeth, whereas in photograph E of
Stodart's cabin there is on the wash basin an ordinary tooth brush
only.   Further, in the inventory of Blane's belongings there
appears a bottle of Gum Tragacanth powder, which is used for
sprinkling upon dentures in order to keep these in position in the
mouth.   As suite C was locked after the crime, Blane was no
longer able to get at this powder, hence his difficulty in keeping
his false teeth in place on the following night.

5.   It will be recalled that, at the end of his first examina-

Police Department.
Form RL/2120/C.7.

tion, on the morning after the crime, the Bishop of Bude fainted.
At that time it was assumed, upon the Bishop's word, that his
faint was caused by a weak heart and the fact that he had had no
breakfast. It is clear, however, that the true reason was the
shock he sustained upon the man, presumed to be Stodart, coming
into the cabin. As the Bishop had not breakfasted with the others
it was the first time that morning he had seen the secretary and,
as he knew him to be Blane, he must have thought at first that he
was seeing a ghost.   The reason for Blane's letter, written from
New York to the Bishop, warning him that some very strange things
might occur once the yacht put to sea, and that whatever might
happen the Bishop was to keep his mouth shut for his own sake, now
becomes apparent.

Blane's confession on his arrest confirms the above
deductions.

John Nilton Schwab

Lieutenant
Florida Police.

CONFESSION OF BOLITHO BLANE.

Yes, all right then, I killed him. Little sycophant, what use was he, anyway?

I've known since last December that I might have to get out any minute. In fact, I suppose I've realised it might have to come sometime ever since I started business. Big business is like that, but you wouldn't understand with your safe little job and pension at the end of it. I suppose that's why I never let myself come in personal contact with my staff, that and the fact I hate people .... most people anyhow.

All I wanted was peace, and I knew if I could find someone to step into my shoes and leave me his to step into I could have it. I started looking in January for someone whom my shoes would fit. It was only a question of patience. Someone of the right height, build, age and with no friends would turn up.

Stodart turned up in Ipswich - - about the fifth place I had spent a week in, advertising and interviewing applicants. He was ideal, no friends, no family - just the sort of man I wanted to become myself, so I decided to let him do the first big thing he'd ever done -- go out with a bang.

When Rocksavage asked me to his conference I thought there was a faint possibility of pulling things together, and Stodart could have gone back to his clerking. By the time we got to New York, though, I knew my position was hopeless and I decided to put Stodart through the hoop.

I had a nasty shock in New York when I learnt that the

Bishop of Bude was to be on board.   Very few people know me by sight and it was rotten luck that one of them should chance to be among this party.   Fortunately, however, I knew more about him than he did about me - a nasty business during the war which everyone's forgotten now and I knew that the Bishop would rather that they weren't reminded, so I wrote him a little warning that there was real trouble coming to him unless he kept his mouth shut.

I don't suppose you want to know how it was all done.   Its pretty obvious now, but if some very bright bird hadn't been a little too clever I should have been in the South Sea Islands by this time.   The details?   Here they are:

I got some closing prices from New York by long distance before coming on board and wrote them in a disguised handwriting I had been practising a long time on a page of my diary.   I wrote a message to Stodart in my own writing on the other side, and put it in my pocket.

As soon as we were on board I gave Stodart some work to do in our drawing room and went to see the Bishop.   I found my note had had the desired effect, and although I told him nothing, I could see that as far as he was concerned I could bump off the whole Church of England so long as I didn't dig up that nasty business out of the past.

Then I went back to the drawing room and gave Stodart a little knock on the back of the head with a hammer I had with me for the job.   He was sitting at the small round table, so I moved the writing table away from the window, and dragged him across to it and popped him out. It was quite dark by then so no-one could see from the deck. Then I threw the hammer and the gloves I wore while I was arranging the room to join him. I found I'd cracked his silly thin skull, so I had to sponge out a spot of blood on the carpet before I changed into evening dress in his room.

I got up to the lounge at half past seven and introduced myself as Stodart and after a while wrote the closing prices in my diary again in front of everyone, and in the same kind of hand-writing. I told the steward to push it under the door of the cabin and stayed in the lounge until the bugle sounded for dinner. The Bishop, who was among the people who came up while I was there, showed he was safe for anything by not turning a hair when he was introduced to me as Stodart.

After that everything went according to plan. At eight thirty the Steward came up with the note I had left addressed to Stodart and I hurried down with him to the cabin. While he was in the bathroom I exchanged the note I had kept in my pocket with the one that had been pushed under the door. That proved the missing party was alive at seven forty-five, and you see although I'd worked this thing out pretty carefully the difference between doing a thing just well and doing it properly is to make allowances for the unexpected. I didn't see why the suicide story shouldn't be accepted without question, but if they did prove a murder I didn't want to be in on it. It's one thing to go down for killing Stodart; it would have been very disagreeable to have been charged with killing Blane.

You know, it's almost worth it to have seen the Bishop's face when he saw me the next morning and realised I hadn't committed suicide.   After thinking he was rid of me he must have realised what I had done.   That's why he fainted.

Well, that's all, and since it hasn't come off I want to see it finished with as little delay and formality as possible.

B. Litton Blane

Witnessed

Kaye Kettering

on S.Y. Golden Gull   10.3.36

Detective Officer

Florida Police